# ELLE HARTFORD

# Worthy in Love

## Pomegranate Café Romance #1

*First published by Phoenix & Kelpie Press 2023*

*First edition*

*ISBN: 979-8-9872017-8-7*

*This book was professionally typeset on Reedsy.
Find out more at reedsy.com*

*This first-in-series is dedicated to the mythical patron of the Pomegranate . . .*

*and to everyone who needs a little reminder that you, too, are worthy.*

# Contents

| | | |
|---|---|---|
| *Prologue* | | v |
| 1 | Fairy Tale Falsehoods | 1 |
| 2 | Little Siblings and Other Disasters | 5 |
| 3 | You've Got Mail? | 13 |
| 4 | Options, Zero | 19 |
| 5 | Best Laid Plans | 24 |
| 6 | A Prisoner Here Myself | 30 |
| 7 | Pleasant Company | 35 |
| 8 | A Conspiracy of Friends | 42 |
| 9 | A Crafty Duel | 49 |
| 10 | Sugar and Spice | 57 |
| 11 | Reckless Abandon | 68 |
| 12 | Gentlemen and Ladies | 77 |
| 13 | Any Press . . . | 83 |
| 14 | Code (Valentine's) Red | 91 |
| 15 | Magic is Better Than Boats? | 97 |
| 16 | Love and Murder | 107 |
| 17 | New Ground | 114 |
| 18 | What I Like About You | 125 |
| 19 | Big City, Small Town | 133 |
| 20 | A Surprise Bidder | 140 |
| 21 | Won at Auction | 146 |
| 22 | Valentine's Magic | 151 |
| *Epilogue* | | 154 |

*About the Author*                                    158
*Also by Elle Hartford*                               160

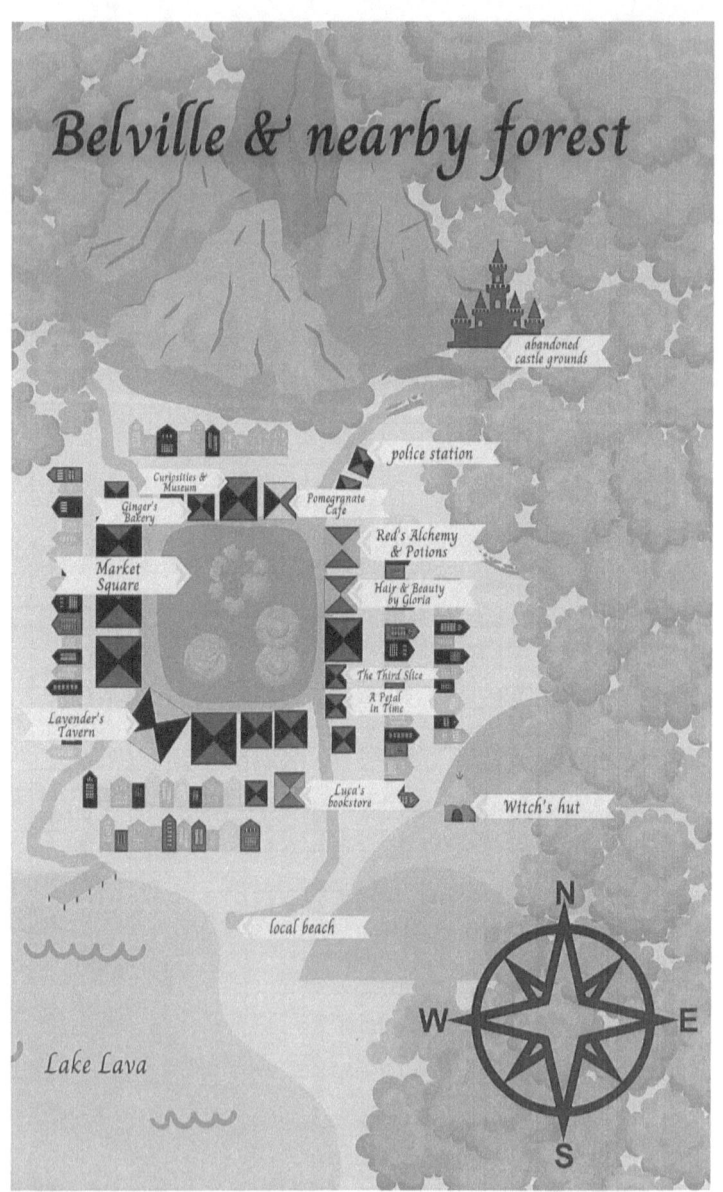

Belville & nearby forest

abandoned castle grounds

police station

Curiosities & Museum

Ginger's Bakery

Pomegranate Cafe

Red's Alchemy & Potions

Market Square

Hair & Beauty by Gloria

The Third Slice

A Petal in Time

Lavender's Tavern

Luca's bookstore

Witch's hut

local beach

Lake Lava

N
W    E
S

# Prologue

## Sakura

Oh, that special stress that comes from putting on a party, or arranging the debut of a new product—or both. Have you ever been there? Putting up decorations the night before, listening to the most upbeat music you can stand, and wondering how in the world you didn't think to check that delivery of the exact thing that you need most to make tomorrow a success, which is now lost somewhere in the inscrutable abyss that is the mail system . . .

Well, in any case, that's exactly where I was when this story starts.

Although, technically, you could say I've been scheming to make my big brother Ryuko fall in love since I was six. That was about twenty years ago now. Back then, I wanted him to marry the lady who sold ice cream cones on the boardwalk at the beach. Seeing as he's a complete spoilsport—and was probably eleven at the time—that particular plan didn't work

v

out. We had to pay for our ice creams all summer.

But this is the time I got it right. I knew I would eventually. (Ryuko may have had his doubts, but then again, doesn't he always?)

Anyway, you don't want to hear about it from me. I'll let Ryu and Mel take it from here!

# One

## *Fairy Tale Falsehoods*

Mel

"I'm so sorry, Sakura," I said, for the third time that morning. "I'll do anything I can to make it up to you, I promise."

If my life was a proper fairy tale, this is where some kindly guardian would have stopped the whole thing. Maybe they would pause time, or put everyone else to sleep, or just shout out from the nearest rooftop: *No, Emmelayne! Never promise a shadow witch that you'll do anything she wants!*

But despite living in a magical world, my life *isn't* a fairy tale, and there was no one looking out for me that winter morning. I was as alone as a stump in a clearing, as my grandmother had liked to say—an expression that tickled her especially because she'd been a forest elf who often described herself as "bark-

1

colored." I'd just moved back to Belville and I was trying so hard to make sure my career as the local postmaster started on the right foot.

And losing a delivery of exotic tea for the Pomegranate Café the week it was supposed to open was *not* a sign of my luck turning around.

But fortunately, for a shadow witch, Sakura actually seemed very nice. I'm not sure really what shadow witches do, but Sakura hadn't once threatened to turn me into a toad or anything. Aside from bright white hair, she looked like an average human twenty-something; but I suppose that's not saying much, since I just look like a normal human with slightly pointy ears and rounded curves, despite my elf heritage. Still, Sakura seemed more like she did sugar plum fairy magic than curses, with her blue eyes and flushed cheeks.

And there's another moment when a guardian spirit should have yelled out, *Oh, Mel, you think so now—don't be fooled!*

But like I said, at the time I had no idea. And I felt *awful.*

"I knew I should have had it delivered directly by the tea company," Sakura was muttering to herself. She was shorter than me, wearing a bright pink apron covered in cookie dough, and when she shook her head, her bobbed hair swung around her face. Most likely she was several years younger than I was, but the fact that she owned a business gave her an air of dignity. She went on, "Oh, but I don't say that as a strike against *you,* Mel. I know you're just starting out and things are hard. I mean, after all—we're kind of in the same boat!"

We kind of were. At the beginning of the new year, just a few weeks previous, I'd shown up in town to take over the local post office. Its previous postmaster had left it in a complete shambles. So I totally got how Sakura, who was preparing for the grand opening of her new café in the center of town, might feel.

*Except none of my work stuff got lost in the mail,* I couldn't help but think. I shifted guiltily from foot to foot, feeling ginormous and awkward on top of terribly irresponsible. Not to mention about fourteen years old, despite having celebrated my thirtieth birthday a few years ago. "That's really nice of you to say, Sakura, but really, it's just unacceptable for things like this to happen. I don't know how well the mail ran under the person before me"—actually the reports had been pretty specific: it ran *abysmally,* and that's why I was here to turn things around—"but this really isn't how I want things to go. I'm determined to make it up to you. Your box will be delivered to you the moment we find it, of course, day or night. Just please, *please* don't say anything to the regional center for Pastoria, not yet, let me handle it—"

"You're worried that I'll report a failure on your part?" Sakura tilted her head and watched me, just for a moment. Then she burst out in a laugh. "Oh, don't worry! And call me Saki, all my friends do. I can call you Mel, right? I'm *positive* we'll find a way to smooth things over. You'll just owe me a favor, that's all."

"A huge favor," I said, immensely relieved that Sakura—Saki—wasn't planning to inform my superiors. A loss like this so early in my tenure could jeopardize my career, and I really wanted this job in Belville. Contrary to what my parents back in New Dale might think.

Saki, meanwhile, was nodding. "Yes, just so. And you know what? This gives me an idea. Maybe tonight *won't* be our grand opening after all."

"You can do that?" I asked. My head spun at the thought.

3

Clearly, I could never run my own business. I preferred the predictable rules of the post office.

"I can if I promise everyone something even better to come," Saki replied, her blue eyes gleaming. "I'll tell everyone I'm delaying opening in order to prepare for a big event. A big *Saint Valentine-themed* event!"

"Oh . . . well, that does sound like a good idea. I think we could find your delivery by then," I said cautiously. Saint Valentine's Feast was an old traditional festival, the kind of holiday that was a big deal in rural places like Belville. It was also only a week away. I hated to over-promise. But I also hated that my failure made Saki feel like she had to delay her opening.

"Don't even worry about the delivery," Saki assured me, clasping her hands. "What I have in mind will be such a hit, everyone will forget all about that tea. We could just serve water and I bet they wouldn't even notice. The café is going to host a *Valentine date auction!*"

Guardian spirit or no, looking back, I think that probably the over-brightness of her smile should have warned me that something *big* was coming. I should have known then that I was already in over my head.

# Two

# Little Siblings and Other Disasters

Ryuko

"Ryu, big brother, are you doing anything? Because I have something even better!"

The moment Sakura called out from the doorstep of our shared apartment, I knew I was going to hate whatever she had in mind.

Sakura would tell you that's because I hate most things. That's not true. *You* try growing up with a little sister like her. Someone has to be the reasonable one.

I mean, I guess given my past—and the fact that I'd ended up working as a part-time shop assistant and sharing an apartment with my adopted sister *and* her strange friend—you could argue that being reasonable didn't get me very far. As a kid I was

5

good at paper stuff, at least. Details and numbers and writing things down, stuff like that. The problem was that when you grow up a snakekin boy in a big city with few prospects, being "good at paper stuff" eventually just means counterfeiting.

I *am* good at counterfeiting.

I mean, I *was*.

Seeing as my skill at counterfeiting only got me in over my head with people I didn't care for and landed me with court-mandated service for one of the companies we swindled, that wasn't something I practiced any more.

These days I couldn't even fake a smile. When Sakura found me slouched over the kitchen table, peeling a winter squash, I grimaced. "Whenever you call me 'big brother,' the answer is automatically no," I said. "Also, your pal Glacial is in the back room trying to nap. You should keep it down."

But Sakura, as usual, was too distracted to listen. I think she has a special filter in her brain that cancels out words like "no" or "should."

Instead, she'd noticed the halves of squash on the cutting board. "Stew again? How very—seasonal," Saki declared, not hiding the scrunch in her nose. Squash soup isn't my favorite either, but I liked to think I made it well. I glowered at her. She cleared her throat. "What if I told you that you could have a really nice, fancy dinner? Actually *two* fancy dinners!"

I continued glaring at her. There's a stereotype out there that snakekin—people whose ancestors had snake-like qualities—are quick to anger. That's not true. For me, being snakekin just means I have scales covering my head instead of hair. It doesn't give me any special benefits. Except an acquired patience. With Sakura, I've found that if you wait long enough, eventually the other shoe drops.

"I'm hosting a big party at the café!" she enthused, grabbing a spoon and dropping into the chair across from me.

Knowing that she planned to help by scooping seeds from the squash, I passed her the half I'd already peeled. "Let me guess," I said. "It's a Saint Valentine party."

"How did you know?"

"Because it's you." I leveled another pointed look at her. Even though we had faced some dark things as kids—like a horrible accident that left her with prosthetic legs, and my misguided descent into crime—Sakura's always been obsessed with stuff like true love. When she was a teenager she disappeared for years, studying magic. Ever since she came back into my life, she's only doubled down on her passion for matchmaking. Saint Valentine's Day, with its love and flowers and other sentimental stuff, was right up her alley. I was honestly surprised she hadn't chosen to open her café on the holiday in the first place.

"Well, I guess that's fair," Sakura said, grinning at me over the squash. "Anyway, it's going to be a really amazing party. I'm going all out. We're going to give out heart-shaped cookies and have lovers' pasta and fondue, and earlier Glacial said she could source some really good wine, and we'll light up the whole café with candles and everything."

I rolled my eyes. If *Glacial* was on board, then there wasn't a ghost of a chance of talking Sakura out of it. Glacial didn't even know the meaning of the word "limits." She probably hadn't ever heard it before. As Saki's best friend and co-owner in the café, she definitely wasn't an ally in my effort to keep Saki practical.

And if Glacial had promised to get wine "earlier," that meant Sakura had already been planning this event all afternoon.

7

"Plus we made these gorgeous invitations using a new ink Red's carrying in the potions shop," Sakura continued. She'd already forgotten about the squash. I reached over and took the spoon from her, continuing to scoop seeds as she went on. "They'll go to everyone in town. Lavender said she'll put up a poster in the tavern if I can get it made by tomorrow. And a few people have already agreed to donate extra items to be auctioned!"

Great, so the local innkeeper was on board too, and who knew who else. How Sakura had managed to charm an entire town in a matter of three months was beyond me. I'd lived in Belville three years, and spent almost every evening alone.

That was, of course, until Sakura moved in, and then invited her friend to join her. *To help with the café,* she'd said. I'd worried at the time that she intended to set me and Glacial up—which would have been a cruel joke, seeing as I'm six feet tall. Glacial'd be lucky if she could top five feet on her tiptoes. Supposedly she was some big mercenary or something before she decided to settle down and bake for a living. She doesn't look it, but she *does* act like it. Except to Saki.

Anyway, luckily, the only joke Sakura'd had in mind was making us spend Yule rebuilding her café from the inside out. If I'd have known all the trouble it'd lead to, I think I would've just stayed home.

When Saki'd been silent for long enough and I knew she was staring at me, I grunted. "You've been busy."

"Well today started out pretty terrible, actually, when Mel from the post office came over to say she'd lost my crème cacao tea," Sakura admitted. "I was getting so upset wondering how I could salvage the opening party, and then this idea just *came* to me, so I decided—"

8

"Back up," I interrupted. "The post office lost your tea? The tea you ordered specially and have been advertising since New Year's?"

"Yes, but slow down," she replied.

Before she could add anything, I said, "*You* slow down. You're the one who's been running all over town planning some huge event. *Another* huge event."

"Yes," Sakura repeated, "but that's your 'who do I need to punch in the face' voice. You don't have to punch anyone! It turned out fine."

The spoon in my hand slipped and dug straight through the squash. "It did *not* turn out fine. You're taking on way too much. Sakura, you know how I feel about this. Opening the Pomegranate is a lot of work already—"

"I've taken on a lot of work, sure, but I'm also not *five* any more," she insisted, getting up to lean over the table and lay her hand on mine. Probably she was afraid I'd start throwing things otherwise. (I *wouldn't* have. Probably.) "Ryu, why is it so hard for you to see that I've grown up? You don't have to look after me any more. I get along just fine."

I snorted. "Says the girl who almost got herself kicked out of town last fall!"

"Those were extenuating circumstances and you know it!"

"Well, this is starting to sound like 'extenuating circumstances' too. Why can't you just take a break once in a while?"

Oh, because the post office sucks, that's why. Just another thing to love about living in the sticks, I guess.

But Sakura wasn't getting a pass on this one, as far as I was concerned. She could have handled the situation in so many other ways that didn't involve giving herself *more* work. I glared at her until she said,

"You know that isn't how it works, Ryu. Starting a business like this is *expected* to be a stressful busy time. That's normal. It's all going to end up fine—you'll see. I just need a little bit of help, that's all."

I figured that this was what she'd been leading up to all along. I'd already spent all my free time over the winter helping the local carpenter basically gut and reconstruct her café. I had half a mind to refuse this additional request . . . but of course I never could actually tell Sakura *no*.

Begrudgingly, I asked, "What do you need me to do? Cook?"

"Oh, no," she said, with a little laugh as she looked down at a mangled half of squash. "Actually, I have something even better for you to do. See, since it's the Valentine Feast, and Saint Valentine's Day is a time for people to get together and start new relationships, I figured, why not turn the dinner into a fun event? And it'll help us raise money for restoring the second floor of the café at the same time! We may even donate extra proceeds to a local charity—I haven't figured that part out yet."

As I listened, my misgivings grew. Money for more construction was good, but I knew Sakura. I could see where this was heading.

"So I remembered those events that would happen sometimes around this time of year back in Brass, you know, the auctions? It's like a game, and people pay money to go on a date with someone! Of course, we'll make sure everything is consensual and in good fun, naturally. But see, that's why it'll get you *two* dinners. The first dinner is the auction itself. Then when someone bids on the date and wins an evening with you, you'll get another dinner—free!"

I sat back and crossed my arms. "No."

Sakura faltered, and I knew exactly what she was going to do. I looked away so that I wouldn't see her eyes get all huge and watery, like she might cry, the way they had when she was a kid.

"Ryu," she said pleadingly. I still didn't look. "You can't say 'no'!"

"I can," I informed her. "And I do."

"But I already put it in the invitations," she said.

That broke my resolve. I stared at her. "You already told everyone I'll do it? What were you planning to do, tie me up and push me on stage?"

Sakura brightened. "I guess that'll work if you won't agree ahead of time!"

"Oh no, it won't," I glowered.

"But Ryu! I've already had to delay opening night once. I can't possibly cancel this auction!"

"Then auction off someone else. *You* do it," I suggested.

"I can't, Trent'd have a heart attack," she retorted.

I gritted my teeth. I'd always thought of Trent, the local Witch, as a pretty cool guy. That is, until he'd decided to develop a massive crush on my baby sister.

"Make Glacial do it," I said.

"I can't. You know what she's like," Sakura said.

Again, I stared. "You're telling me *Glacial* is too grouchy to auction off, but I'm not?"

"Glacial isn't grouchy. She just needs time to open up. You, on the other hand, have had years to open up to everyone in town," Sakura reminded me. "Besides, I already put your name on the invitations."

I gave up staring. Clearly, it wasn't doing any good. *I should have moved out of this apartment the day Saki asked if she could*

11

*move in,* I thought. It wasn't the first time I'd had that regret. But I also knew it wasn't true. There wasn't anything wrong with Saki—even if she *did* like to meddle and jump the gun. The problem was me. If I'd been a better big brother, I probably would have agreed to the auction from the start. Heck, I could have even suggested it. At least then I wouldn't have ruined a squash while hearing about it.

With a massive sigh I gathered up the remains of our mangled dinner and resigned myself to my fate.

# Three

# You've Got Mail?

## Mel

I live in a little cabin on the outskirts of Belville—it used to be my grandmother's, and no one else in the family wanted it after my mom and dad left for the big city. When my mother talks about some relative "settling" in the country, she doesn't mean it like "making a home"—she means it like they've failed to reach their potential somehow. But I like it. It's peaceful, and you can hear birds singing in the morning, and the forest is just a stone's throw away. I'm not especially fond of the forest, even though my family does come from forest elves—I just like lakes and water better, somehow. But I do like the forest a lot better than I liked New Dale, where everyone was loud and alone and hurrying. Out in the forest you might

13

be secluded, but you're never hurried. Whether or not you're alone is debatable . . .

I suppose my point is, I kind of figured that after the whole debacle with losing Saki's box of special tea, I could lie low for a little while. My little house was out of the way and well-stocked, so it'd make a good bunker. Of course, I'm not actually a very good cook, so most of the "stocks" wouldn't do me too much good. I knew *eventually* I'd run into Sakura again, probably when I broke down and visited The Third Slice for a proper dinner (a.k.a. pizza). But I didn't realize I'd be seeing her again *the next morning.*

When I trudged up the path to Belville's post office—my commute from my cabin is about a ten minute walk, which is *not* enough time for my brain to wake up, especially since my work starts at dawn—she and her brother were standing there on the front step. At first I thought I was dreaming.

Except I'd never actually dreamed about Ryuko before. Sakura had been a shadowy figure in my nightmares for a few days, basically ever since I'd realized that her package might be lost. But I'd never even talked to Ryuko, her older—and much taller—brother. He hadn't lived in Belville when I'd grown up, and I'd only been back for little over a month, after all. Plus, he was the kind of person who doesn't make casual conversation easy. It seemed like every time I passed him, he was frowning.

And that morning was no exception. He and Sakura were obviously arguing as I walked up. I know it's a stereotype that the people in charge of post offices are nosy, but I'm actually not. I know everyone's got a lot going on, and they'd probably prefer that most of it was private.

But they were standing *right* in my way, so it's not like I could have ignored them.

And . . . Ryuko is kind of hot.

Obviously, in that way that's like, *this would be a really bad idea.* Those were my very first three coherent thoughts of the morning:

*Sakura and her brother are in my way, and they seem to be real*
*Ryuko is kind of hot actually*
*But of course that'd be a terrible idea.*

The last thing I needed in my life was romance, particularly with a broody man who rolled up his sleeves as he talked and whose head was covered in snakelike scales that actually happened to be my favorite color, purple, and—*shoot,* I realized. *I am definitely not at 100% this morning. I wonder if I can sneak by without them noticing and wanting to talk to me, so I don't make a fool of myself?*

"Hi, Mel!" Sakura called, abruptly cutting off whatever her brother was saying.

Ryuko, I couldn't help but notice, had really nice hands. Pale, but strong. Scattered purple scales crisscrossed over his forearms and disappeared under his shirt.

As Saki stared at me expectantly and Ryuko crossed his arms and I tried my best to act like I hadn't just been staring at him crossing his arms, my hopes for the morning plummeted. Ryuko was now glaring at me. Defensively, I glared back. It's not like I'd lost *his* stuff in the mail.

"Hi, Sakura," I mumbled eventually. "Sorry, I didn't expect to, uh, see you here?"

"I told you, call me Saki. We're friends," the shadow witch reminded me.

Behind her, towering over her in fact, Ryuko snorted. "Friends don't lose friends' mail."

I reeled, and immediately took back all my nice thoughts

about his hands. And shoulders.

"Ignore him, Mel," said Sakura, with a wave of her own hand. "Anyway, I know it's weird, like we're lying in wait to ambush you, right? It's all Ryu's fault, really. I need you to explain to my foolish brother that you already delivered the invitations to my Valentine auction in yesterday's last mail run."

"We already delivered the invitations to the Valentine's Feast yesterday afternoon," I parroted, staring at Ryuko again. *He wanted to come see* me? *Why?* To Sakura, I added, "I made sure everyone got them. Of course, most of the neighborhoods only get the morning mail, so those ones will go out with this morning's run, but everyone in town around the Square should have gotten theirs—"

"Oh, that's just fine, thank you," Saki interrupted sweetly. She turned to Ryuko with her hands on her hips. "See? So you *have* to do it. There's just no other way."

I swayed on my feet, at a total loss. "Sorry, there's no other way to what?"

And now instead of glaring at his sister, Ryuko was glaring at *me.* His dark eyes were a little hypnotic—or was that just the effect of the early hour? "If you're going to lose mail, you could at least be honest about *reading* it."

"I never," I protested, offended. "That's why I was promoted, actually. There's all sorts of spells and charms out these days to protect people's privacy. I mean, I know there've been complaints about that behavior before in Belville, but no one's *ever* had that complaint about *me!*"

"You really can trust me and just ignore him," Sakura told me as she elbowed her brother and cut off his response. "He's just mad because *he's* the prize to be auctioned off at the party. A date with him, anyway. Did I forget to mention that yesterday?

Pretty clever, right? What with love being the whole theme of the night and all."

"I didn't know," I stammered. Then my sleepy brain let loose with what I was *thinking* but never, ever in a million years would have *said,* which was, "Someone'd have to be a real masochist to bid on a date with *him.*"

I blame the early hour. And the fact that seriously, all of this caught me off guard!

Also the lack of a fairy godmother.

Also Ryuko, who had done nothing but malign my professional standing, and who was *still* glaring at me. Actually now he was glaring even more. *Well,* I decided, *fine. Two can play that game.*

"At least I know Belville's latest failure of a postmaster won't be a concern," he remarked, his gravelly voice acid and his shoulders flexing as he crossed his arms again.

"If I were you, I wouldn't be all that concerned about *anyone* bidding," I retorted, flipping my hair over my shoulder for good measure.

"Shows how much *you* know." His eyes were basically tractor beams now. They were forest green, actually, something I could see now that the sun had risen a little higher over the mountains around us.

But I wasn't having it. "Oh? And here I thought I'd been reading up on all the gossip in town," I shot back. "Looks like there hasn't been as much talk about you as you might hope."

Meanwhile, Sakura's eyes had been bouncing back and forth between us like a pair of ping pong balls, her gleaming hair swaying with each remark. "Do you two know each other?"

"No," Ryuko and I said in unison.

"For good reason," he added.

17

"And good riddance," I concluded, not to be outdone.

"Uh huh.  Ryu, come here.  Let's let Mel open up the post office," Sakura said, drawing her brother to one side. I was so relieved I paid no attention when she added, "I've had another idea."

**Four**

*Options, Zero*

Ryuko

I *should* have kept my cool. But it was impossible. Needless to say, I was not interested in any more of Sakura's ideas that morning. Or any morning. As far as I was concerned, she'd gone too far with this auction thing.

And the new postmaster was still staring at me. She looked like she'd walked out of the pages of a fancy brochure about postal careers. Not a hair or pearl out of place. Had Sakura said her name was *Mel?* Honestly, I hadn't been listening. I hadn't come along this morning to make friends with the uppity postmaster who'd caused all this chaos in the first place. I just wanted to settle this with Sakura and then get to work. My actual job, not being the Pomegranate's poster boy.

But the new postmaster smelled really good.

Chalking that up as yet another ridiculous thought all because of Sakura and her constant talk about love, I tried to focus. I really did.

Sakura was babbling about her auction again . . .

. . . and what *was* that smell? Lilac, or something? Some kind of flower.

I guess rude, mail-losing fancy ladies have to smell like *something*.

"And that way, by the time the auction comes around, you can stand up and make a big speech about how you never knew love before and you just wanted to help your baby sister and you tried so hard to do it right but at the last moment, like it always happens in the stories, a *true* love swept you off your feet and now you can't in good conscience agree to a date because your heart belongs to another!" Sakura was saying.

"I'm sorry, *what?*"

It wasn't me who spoke. I still wasn't paying attention. It's not like I have a super sense of smell or anything. I just hate unanswered questions. Also, fancy dress kind of puts me on edge. Blame the old days of city crime, I guess.

So naturally it was the little postmaster who asked that particular unanswered question. Sakura continued obliviously, not noticing how her new best friend had stopped unlocking the post office and was practically plastered to my side as she leaned in to our conversation.

Her shoulder was digging into my arm. She was too warm. Why did *neither* of them see how silly this all was?

"It'll be fantastic," Sakura was saying, still not answering the question in the air. "I'll step up afterward and make a big show of having everyone take a vote. 'Should we hold Ryuko

to his commitment to be our prize? Or should we let him
have this evening with the woman he loves?' It'll be a holiday
miracle—everyone will eat it up!"

"Wait," I said. "*What?*"

"That's what I said," said the little postmaster, stepping
around me. For just one moment, I considered pulling her
perfect chestnut hair, as if we were five years old.

"Oh, don't worry," Sakura continued. "There's no way anyone
will want to hold the auction after that. You'll be off free, Ryu.
Isn't that what you wanted?"

"*He'll* be free . . . by pretending to fall in love with *me?*" said
the little postmaster.

"No," I said.

"How would he even pull that off?" she said.

"I'm not doing anything," I said.

"And what about *my* chances for love?" she said.

"It's not like you'd suddenly be a pariah just because you hung
out with me," I said, annoyed.

My sister, curse her, was nodding along. "That's exactly what
we need—more reason for you two to hang out. That way
it'll look like the romance is blooming organically. Mel, your
family is always throwing big balls in the city, right?"

The little postmaster stepped back from this, like it was some
dirty secret. And of course she stepped right into me. I reached
out to steady her, but I probably should have pushed her into
her post office and locked the door behind her.

She *still* smelled good.

"So," Sakura decided, "you can help with the decorations
when you're done at the post office every day. It'll be a great
way for you to meet more people around town. And Ryu's
already basically in the café as our handyman every afternoon,

21

so he can help you make wooden hearts and stuff!"

"No," I repeated. Although it was pretty clear that no one was listening. Except the little postmaster, maybe. She was probably ecstatic about some new gossip.

She stepped away and shook herself like I was dirty. A reaction I was used to, but it still stung. "Sakura, Saki, really, I'd like to help but—"

"Perfect! Because it'd be a great way to repay that favor," Sakura interrupted with a gleam in her eye.

I groaned. I didn't know about any favor, but I knew that gleam.

"But—why?" asked the little postmaster.

"Because, Mel, if you do this to help Ryu, then it'll help *me*," Sakura explained patiently. She can be very patient when she's getting her way. "It wasn't really right of me to throw him into all this. But you can help me get him out of it and *make* it right! And then we'll be totally square."

"Totally square," the postmaster echoed.

"And I won't ever even dream of reporting the lost mail," Sakura added.

Mel the postmaster pivoted to look at me. I frowned at her. Sakura's words had reminded me why we were here in the first place.

"I need you both to say it," Sakura said. "Come on, Ryuko, this is the only way to save you from going out on some random date. And having to stand up there all evening. And having to dress up. And the two of you can totally get in a fight and break up after the auction is over!"

My eyes narrowed. "Weren't we already in a fight?"

"So, I'm not better than dressing up and going out with some society dame?" said the postmaster.

"From where I'm standing, you *are* a society dame," I replied.

"I need both of you to agree," Sakura cut in loudly. "Or I'm proceeding as planned. And I'm feeling a sudden need for my crème cacao tea . . ."

"Fine," said Mel. She glanced at Sakura, and at the ground, but mostly, she looked at me as she said, "I can definitely pretend to fall in love to repay a favor."

I considered her. She was challenging me. Staring directly into her clear eyes, I said, "Well, *I* can pretend to fall in love in order to avoid a nonsense date."

Sakura clapped her hands together. "Perfect. See you both this afternoon for a decorating party!"

## Five

## Best Laid Plans

## Mel

I've never had an enemy before, except maybe my little sister when we were growing up—for years, we fought like cats and dogs. But she was probably off the list now, seeing as she was happily married and living in New Dale near Mom and Dad, in her own perfect little world. And seeing as I was now at one of Pastoria's smallest post offices, way out on the mountain, it wasn't like I had any coworkers to feud with. Well, technically I did have two part time employees, Katia and Abi, but they had been lovely to me ever since I'd taken over, so they definitely weren't on the list either. And no one else in my family was, either, even though they'd all been a bit weird in the year since my injury—and diagnosis. I guess if you had asked me a few months ago, I might have said my diagnosis was my enemy. But I'd made my peace with it now.

And that meant that the list of my mortal enemies had, at that moment, precisely one name on it.

Ryuko.

And his name was written really, *really* large.

"What's his problem, anyway? I know I messed up, but it's not like Saki was that mad," I muttered to myself, checking the sorted mail with a vengeance later that morning. "She practically ended up saying it was for the best. And what was all that about me being a society dame? That isn't fair!"

Okay, so probably I *do* dress a little more fancy than anyone else in Belville. Being the postmaster means I have a special blue vest, but other than that, I get to wear what I want. I hated society life when we were growing up, but I *do* like clothes that fit properly and use nice materials. And to keep back my hair, which is shoulder-length, I have sparkly or flowery or patterned headbands by the bucketful. Why shouldn't I look nice? No one has as many days as they might wish. So why spend one of them not feeling my best?

That's been my attitude ever since recovery, anyway, and it irked me that Ryuko had misinterpreted it.

Even more because I knew that kid-me probably would have agreed with him. I'd never expected to be a well-put-together career woman.

But my career helped me do things I loved, like live on my own and explore Belville and go paddling on the lake just outside of town. I was already a regular member of Belville Boaters and I was saving up for some home improvements to Grandmother's cottage. I didn't have *time* to waste worrying about Ryuko.

Or meeting with him.

Or pretending to fall in love with him . . .

But I'd promised.

And I really should never have lost that mail.

When the end of my shift came, I steeled myself. Thinking that life couldn't get any worse, I trudged over to the Pomegranate Café, which sat at one corner of Market Square—basically, the center of town, and the center of all town life. And now the center of my own personal storm of guilt and misgivings.

"Hiiii!" Saki's greeting had about five extra syllables as she yanked me in through the front door and shut it behind me. "Gosh, it's cold today, isn't it? The café isn't really open today, so you can sit here," she continued, herding me toward a set of couches in the front corner of the shop. Saki's café was actually really cute and cozy, full of all kinds of decorations I wish I had hours to look at, like the best kind of museum. I would have been happy about spending my afternoon there if it wasn't for—everything else. "You can use the table, too. Oh, and I'll make you some tea! Now, Dusty is going to be by later to drop off some shelves, so you ought to be pretty cozy by then, okay?"

"I thought you said the café hadn't opened to the public yet," I protested vaguely, my head spinning as I plopped down on an overstuffed pale blue couch.

"Oh, Dusty comes and goes as he pleases," Sakura said, waving her hands. "Have you met him yet? Definitely go to him if you ever want something fixed. Or actually, don't. *You* should go to Ryuko. He's gotten really good at carpentry this winter. He and Dusty did most of the repairs in here."

"Really?" I looked around, impressed. I hadn't seen the Pomegranate Café before its renovation, but given how perfect the snug two-story shop was now, I could imagine it had taken a ton of work.

"Yes, and besides fixing things, the other thing Dusty's really good at is gossip. So remember: cozy!" Sakura beamed and skipped off to the kitchen, presumably to make some tea.

*Cozy.* I sighed and sat back into the couch, willing it to swallow me up. If I'd been there alone, it *would* have been cozy. I could snuggle up on this couch and drink warm honeyed tea and read the latest adventure novel I'd picked up at the bookstore and watch the early-spring snow falling out the window and . . .

"Is this how you plan on helping? By taking a nap?" Ryuko's voice, full of derision—seriously, did he have any mode *other* than "derisive"?—snapped me out of my reverie. I struggled upright, meaning to protest, but instead one of my flailing arms nearly knocked over the tea tray in Sakura's hands. I hadn't heard her walk up.

"Oh second thought, maybe you *should* go back to sleep, given your track record so far," Ryuko remarked.

"I was *not* asleep," I protested.

"Play nice!" Sakura chirped, winking at us before gliding away again.

I focused on the tea, determined to ignore Ryuko. Lunch had been some crackers and cheese ages ago, and my stomach was rumbling. Sakura had included some little pastry puffs and sandwiches on the tea tray, but most of them seemed to have creamed crab or smoked salmon . . . *darn.*

"Are you going to touch literally every pastry on that plate?" Ryuko asked.

I flushed. I guess I'd been hoping that if I didn't look at him, he wouldn't be able to see me either. "I was looking for . . .

never mind. It's not like you care anyway."

"Suit yourself." Ryuko, who had taken the seat directly in the window, perpendicular to me, helped himself to a cup of tea before pulling out a small notebook. "So what are we doing?"

But I was preoccupied. "It's not like you can't eat them now," I insisted, pushing the plate toward him.

His eyes narrowed as he glanced from the sandwiches to me. "Are you not eating at all?"

"I can't," I said, and when he sat back, eyeing me like he actually thought I'd poisoned Sakura's pastries, I added in exasperation, "It's the seafood, okay? I can't eat it. I'm—" I waved my hands as if this was an explanation. I'd probably already told him too much. Actually I hadn't told anyone in Belville about what my mother referred to as the "family curse," and I'd kind of been enjoying the anonymity.

"Too bad. The fish is one of the only good things about being here." Ryuko leaned forward and popped an entire tiny sandwich in his mouth.

"Why live here if you hate it so much?" I asked.

His gaze narrowed. "I don't *hate* anything." Glancing toward the back of the café, he yelled, "Saki, your prima donna friend needs different food."

"Be there in a minute," Saki called back from the kitchen.

But I'd had enough. I was already on my feet and halfway to the door. I didn't want to explain myself, and I didn't want to sit around and be made fun of, and it's not like we were going to make any progress anyway, and—

And for the second time, Ryuko interrupted my thoughts.

He interrupted *everything,* actually.

I'm not sure how he did it. One minute I was walking out, and the next minute my back was plastered to the wall and he was leaning over me. I had to look up to meet his eyes. That doesn't happen very often.

And his eyes were really green, and really hypnotic. I guess that wasn't just because of the lack of caffeine earlier, then . . .

"You can't just walk out," he hissed.

"On the contrary, it seems like *you're* the one who can't control his manners," I shot back.

"I thought you were doing Sakura a favor," he pressed, leaning in.

"And if I'd known that her 'favor' would be just an excuse for you to be mean to me, then I would have walked away at the beginning," I retorted. I'm not sure where it came from, but suddenly I felt a tear well up at the corner of my eye.

I hated it. The last thing I wanted to do was show any weakness to this man. But he actually seemed kind of surprised.

"Why should it matter to you what I say?" he asked, without stepping back.

"It doesn't," I said, frustrated. "It doesn't. And I don't have to explain anything to you. This was supposed to be my new start after doing so much to get back on track and go through recovery and I just want to live my life the way *I* want to and that doesn't include wasting time dealing with your ignorant remarks, that's all."

## Six

# A Prisoner Here Myself

Ryuko

I stared at her. Trying to start a new life? Recovery? Living the way she wants to?

In any other circumstance, I might have thought she was lying. Just trying to get sympathy. But her face was so close to mine I could see the gold flecks mixed in with the brown in her irises, and the way that one tear clung to her lashes even though she'd tried wiping it away. Her chest was heaving against mine. She wasn't making any of this up.

"So I'm leaving," she concluded. She sounded defiant, but the words ended with a sniffle.

And that's exactly the moment I decided she *wasn't* leaving. Obviously I was still mad at her for putting Sakura through so much extra stress, and for getting me in the mess too. But she was not leaving.

"Come on," I said, steering her toward the couches with one arm at the small of her back.

She tried to twist away. "You can't just—"

"Listen," I interrupted, catching her free hand. "We can either talk about this while sitting down and eating, or we can keep standing against the wall. Uncomfortably."

"Oh." She stopped struggling, but her gaze on my face was still suspicious. "If you wanted to talk, you should have just said so."

What was I supposed to say—that hearing the frustration in her voice had made me upset too, and sympathetic, and so many other things that there had been no words, and it had been impossible *not* to touch her? Amused in spite of myself, I said, "Oh, so *now* you're interested in what I have to say?"

"If it isn't going to be rude," she replied. She hadn't moved to sit down again. But she also hadn't moved away.

"Ryu's always rude," Sakura announced. She always did have horrible timing, and I swear she had some kind of magical stealth setting on her fairy-made prosthetics that made them make no sound at all. She came up behind us and put a new tray on the table. "I'm sorry, Mel, do you not like seafood? I only went with that option because I thought it might sweeten Ryu's mood. Looks like you two are getting along!"

"Go away," I growled at her.

"Already going," she chirped back. "Don't forget about Dusty!"

But I already had. I focused on Mel. "Tell me your real name."

"Why? So you can make fun of it?" She tipped her chin up stubbornly.

31

"No. Because I hate nicknames," I ground out, resisting the urge to—to what? I'd known her for all of a day. *Curse it.*

"I thought you didn't hate anything," she retorted, oblivious.

"I'm about to hate myself for not letting you walk out the door," I muttered.

"Then why didn't you?"

That challenge in her eyes again. I glowered at her. "Sit down and eat and I'll tell you."

She eyed the tray Sakura had left. "I think I'll take mine to go."

"You will not."

"I will if I want to."

"What's that supposed to mean?"

"Convince me," she said. A small smile grew on her lips as she added, "Convince me that I should stay and help you. Because that's what this is all about, right? I'm just here to help *you*. *You're* the one who really needs me here. So convince me to stay."

If my head had been clear, maybe I would have remembered that she owed Sakura a favor, and she needed this charade just as much as I did. Maybe I would have seen that she was just trying to turn the tables. But it was like I'd forgotten everything that had happened more than ten minutes ago. The force of it was overwhelming. I had to step back from her. Running my hand over my head, I took a deep breath and finally said, "I came here because I was trying to start over, too."

I have no idea where that came from. I'd never said it to anyone. I don't think I'd ever even thought it, exactly.

But she seemed to get it. She kept watching me with those deep eyes until finally she nodded. And without saying anything, she crossed over to the couch and sat down.

32

I took my place again too, but I wasn't sure how to follow that up.

After a few moments of eating in silence, she swallowed and said, "I guess I should be glad you said something. Saki really got it right with these—cream cheese and dill is my favorite. I wonder if she knew that somehow? It's weird how much she knows sometimes, right?" She glanced my way, almost casually, and added, "It's Emmelayne de Foret, by the way. Since you wanted to know."

I *had* asked, but the name made me stiffen. I hadn't expected to recognize it—not the family name, anyway. Everyone knew the Foret family. They were some highbrow forest elves that had had a huge mansion in Belville once, and now lived with the cream of society in New Dale. No wonder Sakura wanted Emmelayne's help with decorations, then. But what was the daughter of a family like that doing working as postmaster? And moreover, what was she doing with *me*? I shouldn't have been allowed within ten yards of her.

"So much for new beginnings with a name like that, right?" she added, and the tension in her voice snapped me back to reality.

"If you don't like it, why use it?" I said, doing my best to keep my voice level.

She seemed offended at first, but then she caught on. I was only parroting her own words to me earlier. She must have seen that, because slowly, she smiled. "I don't use it. Call me Mel. I don't care if you like nicknames or not."

At that, I grinned. She did have style—I had to admit it. "I won't have to call you anything if we don't get these decorations done in time."

"Like Saki would ever let that happen," Mel laughed.

She was right, of course. But there was something else. A light sound in her laughter—a release. A truce. I understood it even though she didn't say a word.

After that, it was easy to design the decorations. To be honest I'd been a little worried, even before I'd known her name. Obviously someone who wore jewels to work at a post office was used to a different class than mine. I'd worried she'd want decorations too fancy, gilded or something—something I couldn't do. But she didn't.

She was, I decided later, too kind for that.

Saki must have told her I was good at carpentry, because everything she suggested could be made of paper or wood. And a little bit of Saki's magic, too. It was like magic, seeing the way Mel threw herself into planning this event for people she barely knew. She smiled as she drew out diagrams and lists. She laughed when I told her we'd need a whole year to make some of the things she suggested.

In the end, I did forget all about Dusty.

# Seven

# Pleasant Company

Mel

"No, do the different sizes of hearts nestled inside each other, kind of like a mobile," I said, reaching over to fix Ryuko's drawing. "Can you do them so they're facing in different directions, you know, like three dimensional?"

"It doesn't matter what *I* can do, because these ones are just made out of paper," he replied gruffly. "And the whole thing was a mobile to begin with."

"Right, I forgot. Paper. And so are the garlands. You really think Saki can get enough supplies in time?"

"I'm not my sister's keeper," Ryuko replied, and then added in a low voice, "apparently, she's mine."

I grinned. "But you *are* in charge of the wooden centerpieces for each table. They have to be sturdy enough to support flowers, but look kind of ethereal—kind of snowflakey."

"I thought the theme was hearts," he grumped.

"The theme is waking up from winter and blooming into love," I retorted. I don't know where that came from; years of listening to my mother plan parties, maybe? I had to admit, Saki—with her love of huge, themed events—was a little like my mother and sister.

"Barf," said Ryuko. "I thought the whole point of the event was to auction me off. So to me, it sounds like the real theme is forced interactions."

"Bound by ties of love," I corrected him, still grinning. Sure, he was being unpleasant, but ever since he'd admitted to wanting a new start too, at least he'd been speaking in longer sentences. Besides, he was actually kind of funny. And it was cute that even though he said he hated nicknames, he clearly put up with them when it came to his family. And now me.

Not that I'd ever admit as much to his face.

Which, it turned out, was rather pretty when he wasn't scowling.

Anyway, I'm sure he would have kept arguing—because why change now, when we'd been going at it for a solid three hours?—but a new voice interrupted us.

"Ties of love tie tighter than steel," a reedy male voice said cheerfully. I looked up in alarm to see a small man, perhaps two and a half feet tall, wearing denim overalls and a floppy cap. A gnome. *This must be Dusty,* I realized, pulling away from Ryuko and his drawings self-consciously.

Or wait—shouldn't I have been leaning *into* him?

"But o' course, when they made that saying, it was about war,"

Dusty continued, picking up a scone that lay forgotten in the middle of the table, and taking a big bite. "Folks going off to war but remembering their loved ones, and what not. Not quite the thing for a tea house like the Pomegranate, then, is it?"

"Not quite," Ryuko said dryly.

"See you took my advice about drawing things out *before* you try making 'em," Dusty said to Ryuko with approval. As I watched them, I could see a sort of mentor-apprentice relationship. It was a little laughable because not only was Ryuko too old to be an apprentice, he was probably two or three times Dusty's height. But it was also kind of sweet. Dusty tapped his head as he added, "Once you've been at it long enough, you won't have to draw anything any more. It'll all be up here."

His cockeyed grin made me laugh, and he turned to face me. "I'm Dusty," he said, holding out one calloused hand, "seeing as this lout's never going to introduce me properly."

"She could already guess who you are," Ryuko muttered rebelliously in the background.

"My name's Mel," I said, accepting Dusty's handshake with a smile. "I've heard a lot about you, actually. I just moved in at the start of the new year."

"She runs the post office," Ryuko supplied reluctantly. I held my breath, but he didn't add anything about losing packages.

"'Bout time they got a fresh face in there," Dusty told me with approval. "The turnover's been, what, four postmasters in two years? Ever since poor Kit died. Course, I haven't been in the place myself since the second-to-last one—he didn't like me much. So I can't speak to the state of things now, but if you find any of the nuts and bolts are unsatisfactory, just ask after me around town and I'll turn up one day to fix 'em."

"Is that right?" I asked, amused that Dusty could afford to do his business so lackadaisically. We were definitely in a different world from New Dale, where my father could hire a specialized plumber or carpenter via magitech and have any problem fixed within an hour. "Well, thanks, Dusty, I really appreciate it. Saki said you had some shelves for her, I think?"

I'd thought I was helping him, but apparently, Dusty had other ideas. He plopped himself down on the couch across from me and peered across the table with a mischievous grin. "Trying to hurry me on my way, are you? Never met a person so eager to be in this one's company."

He glanced meaningfully at Ryuko as he said it, and I gulped. "Oh, no, I didn't mean to be—"

"You'll have to excuse her," Ryuko interrupted. "She can't help being rude. Comes from living in a big city."

"Is that so, now?" Dusty took another huge bite out of his scone.

"It is not. I'm not the rude one," I protested, flustered.

"The evidence says otherwise," Ryuko pointed out.

"Your own *sister* says otherwise," I reminded him.

"We can all agree with her there," Dusty added gleefully. To me, he explained, "Three years living here, and do you think Ryuko ever said as much as a how-de-do to me? Not until his sister showed up and started changing things around!"

"I believe it," I said. I recognized Dusty's manner—the sort of manner I'd more often encountered in wealthy grandparents lounging at parties, swapping stories of their children. And their friends' children. Saki was right: Dusty *did* like to gossip. Deciding to turn that to my benefit for a change, I asked, "What was this café before Sakura took it over?"

"Oh, lots of things," Dusty said, his short legs kicking against the floral couch. "For a good long while it was an antiques shop, of course. The owner got in a spot of trouble—Ryuko here could tell you more about that than me. Then after that it was vacant, and there was not a little damage done, let me tell you. Buildings need someone living in 'em, looking after leaks and rot. The last tenant before Sakura was just in and out, no real help. We ended up gutting the place, didn't we, lad?"

"It looks incredible," I said, gazing again at the polished bakery counter, gleaming wood floor, and the eclectic collection of tables and chairs. The walls were painted and covered in pictures, but above them, a balcony wrapped around the room. "Will the upper level be open soon?"

"Prob'ly not in time for opening," Dusty said. He spoke with a complete comfort with missing deadlines, something I recognized from years working in the postal service. With another fatherly glance at Ryuko, he said, "Got to get this one up to speed on his whittling and sanding before the banister's done. Can't have anyone falling over the edges, now, can we?"

"Definitely not." I grinned, and followed Dusty's glance to Ryuko. His glance back at me was almost . . . bashful. Was he blushing? It was hard to tell under all that attitude.

"Go on, then, Dusty," he said at last. "We can't stay here all night. I have to get home and make dinner."

"Do you?" I was surprised—of course, I'd noticed how darkness was falling out the windows behind Ryuko, but I suppose I hadn't really paid attention. And I have to admit, I was disappointed. Some part of me had been hoping Sakura would make more pastries for dinner.

I looked up to see Dusty watching me thoughtfully. It didn't occur to me until too late that he'd probably misinterpreted my disappointment. But by then, he'd already bounced up off the couch cushions and was ready to head to the door. "Shelves are on the counter," he told Ryuko. "You can hang 'em yourself, and we'll see tomorrow if they're straight. How's that for a deal?"

"Awful, as usual," Ryuko mumbled. But I thought there might be real affection under the words.

Dusty certainly seemed to think so, because with a smile and a wink at me, he disappeared.

"How did he do that?" I blinked. "The front door didn't open."

"No one knows," Sakura called out from the back of the café. "Did I hear him say the shelves are on the counter?"

"You heard everything, because you were snooping," Ryuko replied, and his tone implied, *also as usual.*

"Please. I have better things to do than listen to *you*," Saki said. As she came over to us, I noticed her apron was covered in flour and what seemed to be pieces of flower petals, lending credence to her protest. She stood and leaned on the couch, smiling down at me. "Obviously that doesn't apply to *you*, Mel. But I did want to give you two some space. How'd things go?"

I opened my mouth to say *not bad, actually*, thinking of the designs we'd come up with. Combined with the Pomegranate's natural charm, they'd make for a really nice event—*if* we got everything done in time.

But before I could speak, Ryuko said, "We need to get home."

And I swallowed my compliment, indignant. "Oh, so it was so awful you can't wait to run away?"

"*You're* the one who was trying to run," Ryuko reminded me, standing. "Why don't you and Saki talk about *that*?"

And with that, he was gone. His exit was a lot less mysterious than Dusty's, though. The front door banged in his wake.

"What was that all about?" I asked, my mouth still hanging open.

40

"Oh, we'll figure out in time," Saki said. For a moment she stared after her brother; then she turned to me. "You weren't having second thoughts about all this, I hope?"

I *had* been, of course. All my threats to Ryuko about leaving had been totally sincere. But. . . after talking about the party all afternoon, I *was* really excited about the decorations. I hadn't realized it, but maybe a part of me had missed having big events to look forward to. Or dread. But the café, and Sakura, and even Dusty—they were all so comfortable, and I didn't want to back away from them now.

Much less have to worry about losing my job if Sakura reported my losing her special delivery.

Ryuko would just have to put up with me.

"No," I assured Saki with a smile.

"Perfect," she responded with a smile of her own. "Because tomorrow night, dinner's on me, and you can lead a crafting party of epic proportions!"

## Eight

# A Conspiracy of Friends

Ryuko

I don't hate everything. The truth is that I'm tired. I'm tired of people assuming I'm the same as I used to be, and I'm tired of life always being the same, day in and day out. Most of all, I'm tired of Sakura thinking she's so clever fixing me up with people. Like she's going to fix me. And boy, did she ever pick a doozy with fancy, proper Mel. By the end of that first night, I was starting to suspect that Saki had lost her tea delivery on purpose just to have an excuse to get us together.

Mel was *exactly* the kind of person Saki would want to set me up with. Someone who would insist on small talk and pretending to be interested in things and having parties filled up with hearts.

When, I wondered, would Sakura learn? None of her matchmaking efforts ever work. I don't know what my sister sees in me, but I know for sure no one else sees it. And Emmelayne de Foret with her nice smile and scented hair definitely wouldn't.

Needless to say, I didn't have much patience with Sakura that evening. And none with Glacial either. I'm not sure I could have even said why. At least Glacial was a quiet housemate. Sakura managed to be everywhere I happened to look, which was pretty impressive in a three-room apartment.

I definitely needed to get out on my own.

But what good would that really do me, in the end? I *had* been living on my own, and that still ended with me feeling like I didn't measure up. Not to mention being mad at Sakura without an exact reason.

The next morning, though, I had a reason. It was only one hour into my shift at the curiosities shop before my boss, Priya, came to me about the gossip.

"William stopped in on his way to the bakery," she announced. I was just trying to sweep up the mess of a broken bottle some kid had left, and she cornered me. "He says you've been making friends."

I rolled my eyes. As a boss, Priya is alright. She's probably in her late forties, never been anywhere but Belville, but she hasn't ever judged me about my past—which is more than can be said for most people in town. For the past several months, however, she'd been trying harder than usual to *talk*. Before that it was always 'clean up in the glassware section' or 'this shipment came in and needs to be processed.' Now she wanted to know about my life all of a sudden. I kind of preferred the old way. I mean, how was I supposed to explain Mel?

According to Saki, of course, I wasn't supposed to explain her. I was supposed to be madly in love with her already, or whatever.

"I guess," I said, since Priya was still staring at me.

Priya smoothed back her hair, dyed deep red to hide the gray. It was clear from the look in her sharp, elvish face that she was interested. "And the two of you are putting on a party at Pomegranate Café?" she pressed.

"Just helping Sakura," I said. Everyone in town knew my adopted sister well enough to understand what that meant. Priya had been around long enough to have seen all kinds of characters in town, too. Thinking that gave me an idea. "Do you remember the de Forets?"

"Of course," Priya answered at once. She glanced around the shop. Seeing it was empty, she went on in a low voice, "They used to live here in town, you know. This was years ago—decades, even. Their daughters were still little when they sold that big house and moved to some city—Brass, maybe or New Dale. They used to live in Sunset House—you know it, of course?"

I did. Pretty well, even. I'd first met Red and William, the gossip in question, at a strange party at Sunset House. It was the only building in Belville that could be considered a mansion.

"But everyone knew even then that they wouldn't stay," Priya continued. "The family'd had a presence here for generations, of course. But de Foret's wife—I never could remember her name—she wasn't one for the countryside. Missed her life in the city, they said. And he'd always been a busy boy—no time for rural life, you know the type. They moved years ago. Twelve? Maybe even as many as twenty? But then I heard only last year from Lavender that one of the daughters had been

44

deathly ill. I wonder if that was why they moved away, after all?"

I stiffened. Fortunately, the bell over the shop door rang, and Priya was too distracted to notice my reaction. She bustled off, and I had time to think.

At first I was kind of worried, almost, wondering if Mel knew her sister had been sick. But then I figured of course she must know. But then why would she have ended up back in Belville? Why would she have *chosen* to come back?

I tried asking Priya later, but she didn't know anything else. She didn't even seem to know that Mel was part of the family. I remembered Mel's insistence about using her nickname and decided not to bring it up.

Too bad no one else in Belville could be as discreet.

William, the one who'd been spreading Dusty's rumors, was at the café that evening. He'd obviously come with Red, who's kind of his owner. William's a magical wolf-dog that talks. Red's an alchemist who's always getting her nose into things. Together, the two are worse than the town's police officer. And if you knew Officer Thorn, you'd know that's saying something.

"Hey, Ryuko! Where's your new friend we've all heard so much about?" William panted from one of the sofas as I let myself into the café.

"What he means is, we're looking forward to helping you put on this holiday event. Though I can't believe Saki talked you into it," Red added.

The two of them had identical smiles, I swear. They looked like a pair of judges, watching me from behind cups of steaming tea. But even if they *are* nosy, they're perceptive. Red especially.

I sighed, ran my hand over my head, and finally gave her a small shrug. At least *someone* understood.

Red just chuckled. "We've been roped into helping craft. Gloria's coming too, and Luca's on his way. Saki's in the back with Glacial making something for dinner. If it was just Saki, I might be worried, but Glacial's side of the kitchen smelled quite appetizing."

"Yeah, Glacial's good," I said, sticking to safe topics. "Sakura's getting better."

But of course William interrupted. "None of this is answering the *real* question we all have, which is who is your new mystery girl?"

I would have glared at him, but I knew it wouldn't do any good. "She's not *my* mystery girl," I protested.

"But she is mysterious?" Red looked amused.

"She's not," I protested again. "Honestly, you probably know her already. She's probably delivered stuff to your shop—"

"I heard you were seen sitting in each other's laps," William declared.

"How would that even work?" Red chided him, laughing.

But I didn't find it funny. *Sakura and her plans be cursed,* I thought. "We were *not.* We were just working on something. The plans for the event. We're not together. We've never *going* to be together. Dusty and Sakura are just making stuff up—"

And that's when the door opened behind me, almost hit me, and someone crashed right into me.

*Emmelayne.* I recognized the smell of her hair before anything else. She'd basically done a face plant into my chest. It should have been funny, but holding her up was distracting. And nice.

Not nice—embarrassing. Especially given what we'd just been talking about. I pushed her back onto her own two feet as the door swung shut behind her.

"Who taught you how to walk?" I asked, irritated already.

"Who taught you to stand right in front of closed doors?" she returned, prim as ever.

"Yeah, well, there's a glass pane in the door. You could *use* it."

"There's also plenty of chairs and sofas and *not*-in-the-way standing room you could use in here," Mel retorted. She gestured to the tea nook we'd sat in the night before, and then saw Red and William sitting there.

"Hi, mystery girl," said William, his annoying doggy tongue hanging out as he grinned.

Red swatted him, which was good, because otherwise I might have done it. And I wouldn't have been as playful. "Hello. It's Mel, right?" she asked. "We heard you're in charge tonight."

A second ago, Mel had been flushed—either angry at me or embarrassed to be seen running into me, it was hard to tell. But she straightened and smiled at Red's recognition. She looked sincere. "Mel, yes. And you two run the potions shop. I remember Abi and I helped you coordinate the glass bottle delivery last week when your normal courier was sick. I guess I am in charge, a little, but honestly Saki didn't tell me anything!"

Mel moved toward them, chatting and finishing up the introductions. I stopped listening. I considered going back to the kitchen and giving Sakura a piece of my mind. But then I remembered Glacial was back there, too, and Glacial's *scary* when she wants to be. And that's coming from someone who used to work with criminal mobs in Brass.

Plus, hearing Mel say the word 'sick' reminded me that she'd also mentioned recovery the day before. *Maybe* she *was the daughter who was ill?* She seemed fine to me now. Vivacious, even. Maybe Priya's gossip was wrong. I let myself fade into the background, and watched Mel for clues. She was animated as she talked with Red and William, and even Gloria. That, too, is saying something, because Gloria—the owner of Belville's one and only beauty salon—can be intimidating and "way too cool" in the way Glacial can be scary.

Again, I found myself wondering why Mel was out in the backwoods like this. And when Saki came out in her apron and gave me a look, I remembered I hadn't been holding up my end of the deal. *I should be acting in love with Mel,* I realized, guilty. *But what should that look like, anyway?*

"Don't worry about what it looks like," Saki said, when she'd pulled me aside and I'd put the question to her. "Worry about what it sounds like. Have you said *anything* to the poor girl yet?"

"She's not a 'poor girl,'" I muttered. "I said something when she ran into me."

"That's too long ago, then. You can say something again when you take this to her," Saki said, thrusting a plate full of snack food at me.

I pushed it back. "I can't take her that. There's shrimp on it. She said she can't eat seafood."

"Good. Then *you* can carry this one," Saki said, producing another tray from the nearby counter.

I took it and followed her back toward the crowd. I knew I was already doomed.

# Nine

# A Crafty Duel

꩜

## Mel

Ryuko helped Saki bring out canapes, and I knew I should have smiled at him or said something flirty or in general just helped put on the show, but I couldn't bring myself to do it. The problem was, I'd heard what he was saying right before I ran into him. We'll never be together. I mean . . . it was true, maybe, seeing as we couldn't stand each other. So why did it annoy me?

Maybe because *he* wasn't playing the game, even after I'd committed?

That's definitely what it was. Anyway, I'd been having a lovely time talking to Red and her friends. William looked like a furry black dog, but from the way he used magic to hold small objects and move his cup of tea, it was clear he was a magical familiar. Red herself didn't seem to have any magic, but she'd traveled all over the world, and I really appreciated her efforts to put me at ease. From her black hair and copper skin, it seemed like she must have come from the Shifting Sands, perhaps. She'd obviously settled well into Belville—when the local bookseller, Luca, showed up, the two were adorably sweet. He kissed her forehead in greeting and even though he sat on a different couch, he was always glancing at her during the conversation.

Actually, maybe *that* was why I felt particularly strained . . .

But it helped when Gloria arrived. Like me, she must have come from a family of elves, but instead of hair, she had a massive plume of red feathers rising above her forehead. It was also clear she had no interest in anything remotely lovey-dovey. She was reserved, but I had a feeling right from the start that she'd be a good ally to have.

*Allies! Families!* Inwardly, I groaned at myself. Why did my internal monologue sound so much like my mother?

So, it was in this state of confusion and frustration that dinner appeared. And I definitely ignored Ryuko as he tried to pass me a plate of cheese and crackers. I *may* have even turned my head away and pretended to focus on Gloria . . . who looked pretty skeptical about it all.

*Me, too, friend,* I thought.

I should have known Sakura would never let matters rest like that, though.

"I'm going to stay out here and let Glacial have her kitchen back," the shadow witch announced brightly, perching on the arm of Red and William's sofa. Was it just me, or was her gaze flicking between me and Ryuko? "And now that you're all warmed up and you have food, what do you say we kick things off with a little competition? We'll team up and work on the heart mobiles. The team that makes the best one gets first pick of dessert! William can be our referee and judge. Gloria, I'll work with you," she concluded.

My rising spirits plummeted. I'd been at enough dance parties to know where this was going. Red and Luca were eyeing each other shyly, and Saki was already shooing me out of my seat.

I ended up standing at the end of the table with Ryuko.

"Guess we're a team," I said reluctantly, watching the others set aside the food and pass around colored paper and craft supplies.

"Ironic," was his only comment.

I knew we ought to play nice, but I couldn't help it: I glared at him. "Well it'd be a lot *less* ironic and on top of that a lot less difficult if *you* could mind your manners," I hissed.

"You can lecture me all night, or we could actually get started," he retorted.

I pursed my lips. "Why bother if you're so sure this will all come to nothing?"

"I—" For a moment he looked like he might protest, but I *had* heard him. I held his gaze, and he backed down.

I won . . . but it didn't much feel like it. I plopped down into the one chair at the end of the table and started sorting through paper, leaving him to sort himself out on his own.

The paper, it turned out, came from Luca's bookstore. It was in all shades of pink and white, some faintly patterned, some boldly so. Almost without thinking about it, I started putting together little piles of sheets that I thought went well together. Meanwhile, I snuck glances around our crafting nook. Saki and Gloria had chosen their paper but were struggling to draw hearts. William was eating the last of the shrimp cocktail. Red and Luca seemed to be making good progress . . . if they could stop smiling at each other long enough.

Watching them, I didn't even realize I was sighing until I felt my shoulders release.

*Yikes,* I thought. *Have I really been feeling that tense?*

"You have to have a plan first."

And there was my tension again. Ryuko had pulled up a chair next to mine. I didn't give him much room because I was still upset, but that backfired when he slid up really close in order to lean over the table. "We can use my drawing from yesterday," he continued, pulling out his notebook. "Did you ever decide how many layers it'll have?"

"I wanted to see the paper we'd be using first," I said airily, ignoring the jibe in his voice. I held up the decorative sheets of cardstock, gauging how strong they'd be. "The last thing we want is for the hearts to collapse in on themselves. But we still want them to be big and full."

"Big, full hearts," Ryuko echoed. I could tell he was making fun of me as he added details to his drawing.

But I decided not to let it get to me. "Yes. Don't worry, I'll do most of the crafting, seeing as you wouldn't have much experience with hearts."

Well, okay, maybe it did get to me a little.

"Not a chance," Ryuko growled. "Dusty didn't make me spend all winter sketching stuff for nothing. We do still have hearts in the country, you know."

"I know everyone else does," I replied, making my final paper choices. "My concern is *you.*"

"Because criminals don't have hearts, right?" He took the paper from me more quickly than he needed to.

"*I* never said that. I only meant I think of you as cold-hearted," I said, keeping my gaze anywhere but on his hands by picking out ribbon and scissors. Also, what did he mean, *criminal?* I thought he just worked at the shop next to Saki's. Why would he think I'd assume he was a criminal?

*Touchy,* I decided, yanking on a piece of string as I measured it out.

"Sorry I don't meet your expectations," he said, his voice more growly than ever.

"It's your sister's expectations I'd be worried about if I were you," I whispered back. William was looking in our direction, and I wasn't sure how good magical dogs' hearing might be.

"This whole thing is nonsense," Ryuko whispered back, his nose bumping my ear as he thrust a handful of perfect paper hearts at me.

I blinked, uncertain what to make of any of it. In the end, I decided to just ignore him and assemble the mobile myself, in silence. The room was noisy enough already. And it's not like he was wrong, exactly, but I still couldn't figure out what his deal with me was in the first place, or why it mattered so much, and how again I'd managed to get myself caught up in all this—

"Curse it, Mel." Ryuko's hand covered mine as my fingers slipped while trimming the ribbon, and he caught the scissors. "This event's sketchy enough without you bleeding all over the decorations."

"I wouldn't have bled all over them," I murmured rebelliously. I wanted to pull away my hand, I really did, but his was surprisingly warm. I hadn't realized he'd been watching closely enough to notice if I was about to cut myself. Also, had he ever actually said my name? *He must have,* I told myself. *I probably just wasn't paying attention at the time. Mother always told me that ladies shouldn't daydream . . .*

"Yes you would," he argued, his voice low so only I could hear it. "Don't you ever pay attention?"

I caught my breath, half wondering if he could read my mind, or if he was going to add some reference, like, *this is how you lost Saki's tea in the first place.* That wouldn't have been fair, of course, but was Ryuko really all that interested in being fair? Or, more honestly, was my own guilt interested in being fair? When Ryuko didn't mention it, I decided to let it go. Instead, I cleared my throat and said, "It's hard to craft when your partner is constantly arguing with you."

"Your *partner?*" Ryuko asked, handing me the finished mobile.

I looked up at him to answer, and then realized everyone else was looking at us.

"Done, then?" Saki asked, a giggle in her voice. "Hold it up! William has to decide which one is best. Is everyone ready?"

Obediently, three paper heart mobiles went up around the table. Gloria and Saki's looked a bit bedraggled, like it'd been made by someone only vaguely familiar with the idea of hearts. *Two* someones, I suppose. Red and Luca's was adorable. But I had to say, Ryuko's and mine looked pretty good—especially since I'd picked out matching patterns for the hearts. And hadn't bled on it.

In the end, we agreed that Red and Luca's was the most robust, and they deserved the first pick at dessert later. In the meantime, we set about making decorations for real. Gloria and Saki were relegated to making garlands and streamers, while Red and Luca were approved to continue making mobiles. To my surprise, Ryuko insisted I help him with the centerpieces. While the others made a mess of paper and canapes at our original table, he pulled me over to another, smaller table and drew out his notebook again.

I glanced back at the happy party behind us, then at his focused face. "Did Saki put you up to this?" I asked, leaning in to make myself heard.

"No. You're the one who thinks I can't be trusted to draw hearts," he replied. "And if you want the centerpieces done the way you want them, then you have to supervise. I'm not remaking any of them just because you don't like the shape or something."

"So this really was your idea?" I asked, eyebrow raised.

"I do actually have some of my own," he retorted, returning to his drawings. "Even if I've never been to a fancy dance."

I watched him sketch for a moment. Then, not because I was mad but because I was kind of amused and felt like teasing him, actually, I said, "Are you sure? Because so far it seems like you've needed a lot of help in the whole 'falling in love' department.'"

"That's because I didn't want to do this in the first place."

"But it'd be to your advantage to do it right."

His pencil dropped and he looked down his crooked nose at me. "You don't think I can do this right?"

"Well, I don't think insulting me and almost making me cut my finger is getting off to a good start," I observed.

"I didn't—" He caught himself, and then said, "You know what? Fine. You think I can't act like I'm in love with you? I can. I could sweep you off your feet if I wanted to."

"Big words from someone who's never even been to a 'fancy dance,'" I challenged, using his own phrase—which really wasn't so far from the truth—for my mother's parties.

"Just because I'm not highbrow doesn't mean I can't pretend," he said, his jaw tightening. "It's all an act anyway."

"Alright then, fine." As I echoed his words, I stared directly into his green eyes. They really were *so* pretty, and this time, the hypnotic quality of them wasn't scary—it was distracting, and a little thrilling. "For the next five days until the auction, you'll be a perfect gentleman."

"And you," he said, leaning in so close our noses brushed, "won't even know what hit you."

# Ten

# Sugar and Spice

❧

Ryuko

**M**el was grinning up at me like she thought she'd already won our challenge. I was determined to prove to her she'd got it wrong.

And, luckily, at that moment Glacial brought out several trays of desserts.

"I need taste testers," she said. I almost didn't hear her, and I doubt the rest of the room did either. She doesn't speak up much.

"We won't let you down," Saki promised, immediately getting everyone's attention and taking over. "We'll take two trays here, and one over there for Ryu and Mel. How's crafting going, you two? Ready for a break?"

"Ummm . . ." Mel looked a little disconcerted. She'd been staring at me still, but it didn't seem like a bad thing. In fact, the way she glanced down at my drawings and then blushed at Saki made me grin.

Maybe proving I could be a "gentleman" wouldn't be as hard as I thought.

"Make sure to try everything!" Saki beamed. "We'll pick two for the event. Right, Glacial? Two?"

"Fine," the supposed ex-mercenary-become-baker said. Then she ran off into the kitchen again.

A few minutes ago, I might have envied her. But looking at Mel, I decided that this might be a little fun.

The tray Glacial'd given us had four different desserts. Cupcakes, mini pies, some kind of cake, and some other concoction of honey and phyllo dough. Some forks and a stack of plates filled the rest of the tray.

This, I decided, was an opportunity. I pushed my things aside and went to gesture Mel to sit. But then I remembered: *gentleman.* Instead of just gesturing, I moved around behind her and pulled out a chair.

She was obviously surprised, because she hesitated. But then she tossed her hair back and smiled. "Why, thank you," she said, her voice more polished than usual.

*Okay, so that's how it's going to be. Over the top,* I counseled myself as I took my own seat across from her. Just because I'd never had money didn't mean I couldn't act.

So—how should a gentleman act?

*Probably a gentleman would talk more,* I decided. Mel was watching me like she expected something, so that seemed like a safe bet. I cleared my throat and reached for the plates. "What would you like to start with?"

58

For a moment I expected her to say something like, *look at you, trying to sound all poised all of a sudden.* But she didn't. She looked at the desserts like she was really thinking it over. "How about the baklava?"

I also looked at the desserts. "Baklava" could only mean one of two of them, so I had a fifty fifty chance. I chose the honeyed one, sliding one onto a plate before passing it to her.

She continued smiling at me.

*Curse it,* I worried. *Did I get it wrong?*

"Would you, ah, mind passing me a fork?" she asked finally, chuckling slightly.

Was she laughing at me? I couldn't tell. At least she wasn't laughing because I'd given her the wrong dessert.

I handed her a fork and took one for me, then turned my attention to the little pastry. It was *really* sweet. I tried to keep my face blank, because I was pretty sure gentlemen are supposed to be impassive. But Mel must have seen something, because she laughed again.

"I love baklava, but I guess it's not for everyone," she said. "Why don't we try the cake instead?"

"Fine." I didn't want to admit it, but the warmth in her eyes was kind of nice.

As I passed her a piece of cake, she kept talking. "Am I right in thinking that you gave me the cheese platter earlier on purpose? Instead of the shrimp?"

Honestly, I was surprised she gave me that much credit. But it *was* true. "Yeah, Saki wanted me to carry in the other one, but after what happened yesterday . . ."

"I appreciate that." Mel paused, and I wasn't sure what to say. So we just sat there eating cake for a moment. I honestly couldn't tell you what kind it was. Eventually she added, "Do you want to know about it?"

My first impulse was *do you really want to tell me?* But then I reminded myself I was supposed to be a gentleman. I was pretty sure that along with being impassive, gentlemen were supposed to never be surprised. Besides, she didn't look reluctant. I straightened. "Why, of course, my lady."

She giggled. "You don't have to call me that. I'm not actually a lady. Actually, I think my great-grandmother might have had a title, but these days my family is just known for their connection with News and Media Incorporated.

"But you knew all that already, I bet," she added. Instead of sounding proud, she sounded a little ashamed, and embarrassed. "I'm just babbling. It's a bad habit, not very ladylike. But then, I guess I'm not the one who said I would act like a gentleman, am I?"

She chuckled, and she was looking at me like she needed something, like somehow what she was saying wasn't what she meant. Maybe I should have stayed impassive, but I nodded and smiled at her.

"Thank you," she said, more quietly. Before I could even guess at what she was thankful for, she went on, "It's just, I haven't told anyone in Belville yet. I haven't had to tell *anyone*, actually, because it all kind of blew up at the time, and with the way my family is . . ." she waved her hands. That I could follow: it made sense that a high-society family in charge of a media empire liked gossip. Or had an interest in hushing gossip up. "Anyway, I'm allergic to seafood.

"It sounds kind of silly, right?" She paused, but she didn't laugh. "It's not like some big secret. Everyone makes it so complicated. My family does, I mean. There's this whole big story in the family lore about how some great-great-grandmother spurned a merfolk lover, or who knows what she did, really, but the story is that she was cursed with this deathly seafood allergy as a result. So some of the women on my father's side of the family have this. But not *everyone* does, and the thing is, it doesn't show up until later in life.

"So I guess it just feels like a big deal because my mother was always so determined that I *wouldn't* end up with it," Mel added, looking down at her plate. "She never said as much, but I'm pretty sure it's why we moved to the city. Part of why, anyway. To do all the doctor visits and whatever preventative trend was all the rage in the papers. Honestly, by the time I was on my own, I was so tired of thinking about it that I *didn't.* I just threw myself into work instead."

She didn't look up until I cleared my throat. "Why'd it matter to her so much? If you weren't even sure you'd get it?"

"It's an imperfection," Mel answered wryly.   But then, thoughtfully, she added, "That's really not fair. I think she really was worried. It's probably not a curse or anything, but it *is* a late-onset deathly allergy. That's all the doctors could tell me. I mean, you can kind of understand why she was worried, when you know that I found out I have this allergy because I was eating my lunch on the go at work and there was fish in the dressing on my salad wrap and I ended up passing out in the street and being run over."

"Excuse me?" *My gods,* I thought, *she can bury a lead even better than Sakura. The two of them could drive a person to an early grave.*

"Erm, yeah." Mel had the grace to look abashed, but she smiled too—probably at my reaction, which definitely wasn't impassive. "Just over a year ago now. It took a long time to . . . well, to figure everything out. My hip was really badly injured, and I had to stay in a rehab center. I still do exercises and things for it at home. Plus it took us a while to figure out what had really happened and why I collapsed in the first place."

"Sounds obvious to me," I said, trying not to picture a half-eaten wrap lying on a city street. I'd totally forgotten about Glacial's desserts.

"Yeah, in retrospect," Mel agreed. "But it was hard to tell at the time because I was also pretty stressed. Just about work and life and all."

"Stressed enough to pass out in the road?" I asked, incredulous.

Mel just looked at me, and I had to swallow the rest of my words. For as much as I wanted to say that so much stress was *wrong*, I knew I'd seen it before. Felt it, even. *You're wearing down*, Saki used to tell me, back when I first started taking counterfeiting jobs. *One of these days something will break, and then what will be left of you?*

"Obviously it wasn't healthy," Mel said. "I didn't even realize it then. I thought putting so much pressure on myself was totally normal—required, even. Like I *should* be running hard at work and always thinking about how to improve. If I didn't do that, then what good was I? Then one doctor told me that everything—the stress, even the allergy—it was all in my head. Like that meant it wasn't real. But then, that's where most of our lives happen anyway, right?"

I had to stare at the unfinished centerpieces on the table, because I knew my face probably looked murderous. Big city doctors were suddenly at the top of my 'punch list,' as Sakura would call it. But that wasn't helpful, especially since no doctors were present. *And some of the doctors must have been intelligent,* I reminded myself, *since Mel is sitting right here and she seems*

62

*fully functional.*

Still, I wasn't sure what to say. But I could relate to life happening in the head. That's where preconceived notions are, and those are what give me trouble . . . For a moment I actually considered saying that.

But she was blushing as she went on, talking about how she was fine and she didn't want anyone to worry, and waving her hands around in this really unassuming way. I didn't want to break the spell. I finally noticed that her plate was empty. It gave me this wild idea. I decided to go for that instead.

"Well, either way, you're lucky most desserts are safe," I told her. "Because I don't think Glacial would accept any excuses for not taste testing."

"I have heard a lot about this mysterious Glacial, but we've barely spoken," Mel admitted, her grin widening as she played along. She seemed happy to change the topic of conversation.

"Most of the time she's fine," I assured her. "But you don't want to be on her bad side. Which you definitely would be if you didn't eat all these desserts. Then I'd have to protect you."

"And would you?" Mel asked, looking amused.

"Of course I would," I said. Maybe a little too quickly. I coughed and got back into character. "Isn't that what a gentleman should do?"

Something flashed in Mel's eyes, but then her smile came back. "I suppose so."

"But as one of my friends used to say, you have to pick your battles," I continued more confidently. "So, with that in mind . . ."

I picked up one of the spare forks and cut into one of our forgotten cupcakes. Then, before I could think or second-guess myself, I held it out across the table.

Mel's eyes went wide and surprised for a moment. Her gaze slid up from the fork to me, and I could have sworn that the temperature in the room rose. Somehow, though, I'd known she wouldn't back down from a challenge.

Gingerly, she accepted the piece of cupcake. For just a moment I thought I could feel Saki's gaze in our direction, but I ignored it. This, with Mel, was suddenly a lot more compelling.

And it wasn't just about the challenge, the game of being "fancy."

Or was it? *Should it be?*

Mel laughed, a little self-consciously, and the rest of the evening passed in the blink of an eye. I was honestly surprised to look around at the end of the night and see that not only had we polished off Glacial's desserts, we'd managed to assemble several centerpieces. We weren't done with everything that needed to be done before the auction. But for once, I wasn't feeling so bad about that.

And for once I didn't feel awkward bidding Red and William and everyone else good night. Mel was there next to me, and she was so personable it was hard to worry. Because that's what I'd been doing before, without even realizing it. Worrying about what they were thinking of me as soon as they turned away.

Instead, Mel turned toward me, and she was grinning. "I guess I'd better follow everyone out. Are you sure we've cleaned up enough here, Saki?"

Of course. *The perfect lady would also be a perfect guest,* I decided. But the thought was more amusing than annoying.

"Of course you have," Saki said, beaming. "After all, we're not open yet, so why worry about a mess? And you'll be back here tomorrow afternoon to oversee any more crafting, I hope."

"Yes, I—I suppose I will," Mel said, glancing back up at me.

"But let's let tomorrow's problems stick to tomorrow," my nosy little sister continued. She was *also* looking at me, but that was more ominous than anything else. "Let's focus on tonight. Ryu, why don't you walk Mel home?"

Mel protested. "Oh, really, I'll be perfectly fine—"

"With me," I said, looking at her meaningfully. "What kind of gentleman lets a lady walk off alone?"

"One who respects her competency?" Mel suggested.

"But not one who values her company," I returned, grinning. Honestly, I don't know where it came from. But it was too good not to end the conversation. I swept Mel out the door before anyone could say anything else, leaving Saki behind us, probably puzzling over the "gentleman" thing. I'd be hearing about that at home, I knew. But I set that aside.

"I have to admit," Mel said, chuckling as we left the café behind, "that was pretty good."

"Told you I could sweep you off your feet," I reminded her.

"At this rate, I'm curious to see how you'll keep it up for the next few days," she said, her breath coming in clouds in the night air.

I settled into walking the streets beside her. "Are you saying you don't think I can?"

"I never said that," she pointed out quickly. The tension eased a little and she added, "Lots of things about Belville have been surprising."

I had to admit I was curious. To me, the little town was boring as dirt. "Like what?"

"How lethal the postmaster job is, for one thing," Mel said with a laugh. "I knew I was cleaning up a 'wayward' post, as my director in the postal service called it, but I had no idea just how 'wayward.' But also just how kind the people are here, too. I guess I—maybe I *did* live in the city too long. Like you're always teasing me about," she said with a smile. "And you. You've been surprising too."

"I bet." I shifted uneasily again.

She nudged my arm with her shoulder as we walked. "In a good way," she said quietly. "Thank you for listening to me earlier. I guess I—I don't know, maybe I thought I'd just hide that part of myself forever. I really wasn't expecting to find someone else interested in making a new start. I mean, not necessarily together," she added hurriedly. "That came out wrong. Though I guess that's what it's supposed to look like. Oh, I'm confused. Do you find this confusing too?"

I watched her for a minute, thinking. Then, slowly, I smiled at her. She deserved the truth. "Yeah, I do."

"But I'm sure you find it much less confusing than I do," she said, nudging me again.

"Naturally," I agreed. "Because I'm a perfect gentleman, and gentlemen are never surprised."

"Really? Maybe I would have known that if I wasn't such a country bumpkin at heart," Mel laughed. "Here, mine is up at the corner. You don't really have to walk me all the way home. We're close enough."

"What," I asked. "Scared of me finding out where you live?"

It came out without any thought. It was just natural. But maybe I shouldn't have said it.

"No," she said. "Why do you keep thinking I'll somehow think the worst of you?"

I faltered. "Don't you?"

"Well, I didn't," said Mel. But she paused. "Unless there's something I should know?"

"There isn't anything."

"Because I've shared with you, so you could—"

"There's nothing," I insisted.

"Then why—"

"Alright, maybe you were right," I said, pulling up. "This is far enough. I'm sure you're competent enough to get home from here."

Mel stopped too, and her eyes narrowed. "Meaning you're tired of my company."

"Or just tired," I retorted.

"Or just opaque," she said, tossing her hands in the air. "Fine, then. Goodnight, Ryuko."

It stung a little that she could still be polite and I hadn't even made it a whole evening. I made myself reply. "Goodnight, Emmelayne."

As I walked away I knew I'd made not one, but several mistakes.

## Eleven

## Reckless Abandon

Mel

After the crafting party, Saki came and found me the next day while I was on my postal route. The postmaster before me hadn't delivered mail, apparently—he'd stayed at the station and made Abi and Katia do both the morning and afternoon routes, along with all the special deliveries. But even in rural Belville, there was a lot of mail to go around, and a thriving local paper to be delivered. I'd made it a point to be involved in the "on the ground" work. Somehow, Saki must have known this. She made it seem like a coincidence, like she was coming back from an errand and just happened to bump into me, but I was pretty sure from the way she said it that she'd actually memorized my routine.

Which honestly wasn't such a bad thing. It was a little flattering even. And it was probably good, because after the confusion of my evening with Ryuko, I might have tried abandoning the whole scheme if Saki hadn't tracked me down.

I didn't tell her that, of course. But I'm pretty sure she guessed.

"I've just come from the grocer's," she informed me, keeping up her cheerful chatter as she fell into step. Over her pink Pomegranate Café apron, she wore a shockingly purple overcoat. In my vest and standard peacoat, I felt a little underdressed. "I was looking at what flowers he had in stock there. I tried A Petal In Time, too—that's the florist down the street from Red's—but they were awfully expensive. Well, it *is* only just barely the beginning of spring, after all."

"Hothouse plumeria," I said, a bit absently. "Or bleeding hearts with fern accents. That's what my mother would use in all her Saint Valentine parties, I think."

"Mel, you're a genius," Sakura enthused. Before I could remind her that it was my *mother's* party-planning expertise that had been my inspiration, she went on, "The florist should definitely have ferns this time of year. And I think Red's been growing plumeria for her anti-pest potions. She must have at least half a dozen plants. Maybe she'll donate some for the event. Have you been in her shop? It's great. Anyway, do you know what's up with Ryu?"

"Ryuko?" I repeated his name to buy myself some time—and try to get my sudden blush under control. "Um, no, why?"

Sakura tilted her head from side to side, pausing on the sidewalk as I stopped to deliver some mail. "Nothing exactly. He's just in more of a mood than usual."

"My impression was, he's always in a mood," I couldn't help

69

but say. Fortunately for me, Saki found it funny. She laughed as we started walking the perimeter of Market Square again.

"I know what you mean, but not that kind of mood," she said. "That's not what I meant. Anyway, you have to cut him some slack. It's not easy living with me for a sister, after all. *And* living with Glacial too, since I promised her I'd put her up until she found a home in Belville. We've kind of taken over his house. I thought it might be good for him, but then, I *am* part of the problem, remember. Plus, not everyone was nice to him when he first got here. Of course, he wasn't especially nice to everyone either, but sometimes it's hard to remember who was cold first, isn't it?"

"I can see that," I agreed, smiling down at her. "So what's wrong with his mood now, then?"

"He seemed especially broody last night. And then he left this morning without a word," Saki said, unbothered as I stopped for another delivery. "You know, it's a bad idea to guess what other people are thinking, but he's probably just frustrated at me. He has a habit of worrying that I'm setting him up," she explained, when I rejoined her on the sidewalk with a curious look. "I may have done that in the past. Once or twice. But this isn't at all like that."

"Right." I hesitated. "Because—you're *not* trying to set him up, right? Not really."

"We're not little kids any more," Saki said. It wasn't quite an answer, but her pleasant manner made it seem like it might be. "If he's got something on his mind that's eating at him, he'll just have to deal with it himself. And express it himself."

"Does he do that often?" I asked skeptically, thinking of how often he'd clammed up on me the night before.

"Oh, self-expression is funny," Saki replied airily. "People do it without even realizing what they've done."

I wasn't quite sure what to say about that, and I was saved from having to say anything at all, because we'd just pulled up outside Lavender's Tavern. The tavern was always busy, with out-of-town guests staying on the second floor and all kinds of travelers and locals in the bar below. I'd started making it my last stop of the day, because there was always more mail to be picked up there—and lots to be delivered, too. It kind of felt like Lavender and I just traded bags full of packages and letters.

But of course, I was a little more orthodox than that. Especially after having lost Saki's tea. I took my time to go through the addresses, and to chat with Lavender, too. It helped me feel at home in Belville. And even more importantly, it reminded me that I really had no reason to hurry. No one was timing me or expecting a speedy performance, not here, not on this quiet mountain.

When I came back out to the Square, Saki was still standing there waiting for me. She smiled, and I smiled back. As frustrating as her brother might be, I realized, Sakura herself was starting to feel like a friend—something I hadn't really permitted myself since my accident. Or honestly, even before that.

"So, what are you doing now? Do you have to go close the post office?"

"Oh, Katia has already done that," I said, feeling so comfortable there in the early spring air in such a quaint little town, with a *friend.* We started walking across the Square, slowly. "I usually just drop off this mail there on my way home, then change and—well, on boating nights I go down to the lake and join the club meeting there, and once a week there's the evening hiking club."

"You should make Gloria join that," Saki said approvingly. "Do you like having all those meetings and clubs?"

"Of course," I answered. But I did think about it for just a moment, too. Joining organizations and going to social events had always been part of my life—my mother and my father, too, were big proponents of community. I'd always thought it was a bit silly, until my injury. Ever since I'd been in recovery, social things started to have new meaning. I'd realized I wanted to get out and live my life, and I couldn't do that by sitting alone at home. "I'm looking forward to when they pick up more, later in the spring," I added. "But for this week I told everyone I'd be helping with the auction, so they know not to expect me."

"Perfect," Sakura said, grinning. "You should definitely invite them all to the auction, too. And in the meantime, just think of our work like a crafting club!"

I chuckled. "Sounds good. Are any of the others planning on coming over tonight? Or Ryuko?"

"Ryu's already there," Saki said, and for a moment I could have sworn she winked at me. "I left him and Dusty finishing up the details on the sales counter. They said they might put up the rest of the centerpieces if they had time, so you could look over them. But—" Her voice faltered. "Isn't that Dusty running toward us?"

She stopped, and I stopped next to her. I hadn't ever seen a gnome run before, and the sight might have been comical if it hadn't felt so ominous.

"Sakura," he called, skidding to a halt in front of us. "Good thing. Weren't sure where to find you. Your brother—in a bad way. In the café."

Dusty was panting pretty heavily, despite the short distance he'd made it from the Pomegranate. Fortunately for him, Saki didn't require any more details. She set off running toward the café, her magic sparkling around her, ready for anything. I didn't have magic and I wasn't totally sure if I'd be welcome, but I decided to follow along anyway. I wasn't busy, and I might be helpful, and—well, I *was* a little worried.

When Dusty and I caught up to Saki inside the Pomegranate, the place was in an uproar. Wood and debris cluttered up the tables across from the sales counter, and magic sparks were flying everywhere. Sakura stood in the middle of it all, arguing violently with a tall young man I recognized as the town Witch, Trent.

In the din and dust, Glacial sidled up to me and Dusty. I felt like I was seeing her for the first time, which was almost true. She was a few inches shorter than Sakura, with light blue skin and purple hair, a sight that my brain refused to process amid all the chaos. "Everything's basically handled," she murmured. "Saki's just a little mad at Trent."

"Mad at Trent? Why would she be? What happened?" I asked. My eyes were fixed on Ryuko, who sat glumly at the center of the scene, his head in one hand. He wasn't unconscious or bleeding, so that seemed positive. But after spending months in recovery, I recognized the signs of someone whose body is in shock.

"It was Trent's idea to try to get the upstairs done," Dusty said. I almost had to bend down to him to hear him as Sakura continued yelling, her back to us. "Wanted to use magic to hurry things along."

"She's always telling him not to do that," Glacial added. "But on the other hand, he *did* just heal Ryuko. Mostly."

"Mostly?" I echoed, alarmed.

"The lad's good at healing," Dusty commented, presumably about Trent. "He ought to stick to that. Leave the banisters and construction to us that know it."

"Ryuko fell through the banister?" I asked, trying to put the pieces together. My gaze finally drifted upward, to the balcony. With horror, I saw that there *was* a large hole in the partially-completed railing that lined the second floor.

"He just wanted to have it done in time for the auction, for Sakura," Glacial said, rather unexpectedly taking Trent's side.

"She knew it wouldn't be done, and that was fine," Dusty argued.

My gaze fell back to Ryuko. I wasn't any good at construction or healing others, but I *did* know how difficult it could be to be injured or ill and unable to get any peace. "I'll take him home," I decided.

As I stepped forward, Saki looked back. Everyone seemed to be staring at me all of a sudden. "Good," she said, which was a relief, because I was already at Ryuko's side. "You live all on one floor, right? Take him there, that'll work. I'll stop by in a while. Once we've finished cleaning up this mess," she added, with a ferocity that made me really glad I wasn't Trent.

I stared down at Ryuko, still processing. I hadn't really thought through whose "home" I'd been referring to. *One floor? My place? What did I get myself into now?*

It turned out that Ryuko couldn't use his left ankle—or his left wrist. This begged the question what the state of his injuries must have been *before* he was "mostly" healed by the village Witch, but I decided not to think about that too much. Or about the fact that he must have fallen right into a table and chairs. Instead, focusing on the present, I got him to drape his arm over my shoulders so I could help him walk out the door.

"We aren't really going to do this all the way to your place, are we?" he grumbled once we were outside.

"Well, we can go back in and ask one of the angry, arguing witches to make you a cane or something," I said, huffing a little under his weight. My own hip wasn't too pleased with this additional burden, but I did my best to center myself, remembering the good practices I'd been taught in recovery.

"Wouldn't be able to use a cane," Ryuko huffed. "Because of my hand."

"Then you're stuck with me," I told him. "Too bad. It would have been very gentlemanly."

He chuckled at this, just a little, and the sound was reassuring. It made me feel lighter. After that, it actually wasn't so bad, getting to my cottage. It did feel like a much longer walk than usual, but it was probably shorter than trying to get him to his own apartment. Sakura had mentioned living on the second floor of a house at the other end of town, and I shuddered to think of trying to get Ryuko to navigate stairs.

No, it definitely was the best idea to take him to my place. I didn't hesitate at all when we turned up the walk, or when I unlocked the front door and helped him take a seat on the sofa. But after I'd gone back to my room to change and I had a moment to think things over again, I did falter a little. Three thoughts chased themselves around in my mind:

*Ryuko is injured.*

*Ryuko is in my* house.

*When was the last time I actually cleaned? Or went grocery shopping?*

Well, none of those thoughts were all that helpful. I finally shook them all off and went out to see what state he was in.

"So." I sat on the arm of my one armchair, a place I usually curled up to read. It rested under the front window, while Ryuko was sprawled on the sofa that took up the wall next to it. In my cottage—which was still decorated very much in the style of "grandmother," with floral wallpaper and faded upholstery—he looked distinctly uncomfortable.

"So," he replied, rubbing his good hand over his scaled head. "I'm probably getting sawdust all over your couch. Sorry."

I couldn't help it: I laughed. "Honestly? I don't care about that, Ryuko. I was thinking more about *you*. How are you feeling? I mean, obviously Trent didn't fix everything . . ."

Ryuko stared at me for a moment, then shrugged, almost bashfully. "He did enough. I'll be fine. I'm just sore. And he said I ought to stay off my foot for, like . . ."

When his voice trailed off, I thought of what Sakura had said earlier, about self-expression. I thought I recognized the look in his eyes. And for once, I felt nothing but sympathy for him. "It sucks, right? You had plans, and now everything's upside down."

"Yeah." His gaze on me was thoughtful, and his smile was slow and crooked, but it felt sincere. "I guess the same is true for you."

"Luckily for you, I know how to make the best of it," I informed him. "I'm not a great cook and I don't have any meat in the house, but I *do* have drinks. Magical healing doesn't mean you can't have wine, does it?"

He blinked. "You're going to drink with me at three thirty in the afternoon?"

I grinned. "If ever a time called for it, it's now, don't you think?"

He grinned, fully *un*-crookedly, in answer.

76

## Twelve

# Gentlemen and Ladies

Ryuko

**M**el wasn't lying when she said she had wine. It had to be some of the best stuff I'd ever tasted. That said, I hadn't actually had any alcohol ever since I'd moved to Belville. I had made a pact of sorts with Sakura, after seeing how drinking every night got to other folks in my situation. Even after they'd done their service and could start new, the drinking would hold them back. I'd promised Saki I wouldn't make that mistake, but to be honest, it was the easiest promise I could've made. For some of my old friends, drinking was a true problem. It hadn't ever been that way with me. My problem was in my head, and drinking had only ever made me sad.

I guess the point is, my tolerance must have been low. Any twinge I felt about breaking my promise to Saki was immediately drowned in my annoyance with her over the Pomegranate. Beyond that, I don't even remember how Mel and I got started on talking about gentlemen. Probably, she made fun of me—or maybe I was trying to impress her. Somewhere into the first cup of wine, I'd forgotten about my injuries. Somewhere into the second, Mel had moved onto the couch with me, and we'd started playing this game.

"Okay," she said, hiccuping. It was adorable. *She* was adorable. I hadn't realized ladies could be so adorable. I hadn't even realized I liked that kind of thing. "If I was drowning, what would a gentleman do?"

"Easy," I replied. "Save you, first of all. Then give you the breath of life or whatever."

"It's called mouth to mouth," she said, and even though she was correcting me, I didn't care. I liked the sound of her answer even better. In her prissy but practical way, she added, "Anyway, that probably wouldn't be necessary, because the boating club keeps lots of revising potions on hand. Reviving potions. I meant 'reviving.'"

"Well, *anyway*, how likely would it be in the first place?" I pointed out, tipping my nearly-empty glass at her.

"Oh, very," she answered with an entirely straight face. "It's just a matter of stat—statistics. I mean, of course you have to be careful. I'm always careful. I do the whole pre-launch checklist and everything. But I'm down there usually two nights a week. Usually. When I don't have crafting club—that's what Saki said to call it. Did she tell you that?"

"You're at the lake two nights a week?" I asked, ignoring any reference to my sister.

Mel nodded and took another long sip of wine. "I love it. Paddling. You have to try it. A gentleman should know how to boat."

"Yeah. Sure. How do you even find time for all this stuff? Is it really worth dealing with all the people?" I hadn't meant to ask that second question. But obviously it slipped out, because Mel laughed. She almost spilled her wine.

"Some of them are really nice," she assured me. "Really nice. A lot of people in Belville have been great. The people who aren't—I just ignore them. Who has time for them?"

This was obviously a rhetorical question, but the wine had me feeling thoughtful. "What if someone challenged me to a duel over you? What would a gentleman do then?"

She snorted. "People don't duel anymore."

"A gentleman probably would," I said.

Mel drained her glass and nodded philosophically. "Okay, fair question. So you think the answer is that a gentleman would duel. Well, *I* would say that a true and modern gentleman should know better. He *would* know better, I mean. Like to let me handle it. Because in these matters, where two people are talking about someone else, is it even really fair, since the first person never gets a say—and what *would* they say, you know? We don't know, because they never get a chance. Isn't that the real tragedy?"

"Not if I died," I pointed out. "I'd like to think *that* would be the real tragedy."

She rolled her eyes, her hands waving. "People don't die when they duel. Not any more. Because they don't duel. Next question."

"I thought you were asking the questions," I protested. Rather than come up with another question of my own, I pushed the bottle on the table a little further away from us, where we couldn't hit it accidentally.

"What if I wanted to kiss you?" Mel asked suddenly.

My hand jerked, but I didn't even notice if I'd knocked over the wine. Her eyes were so big. Was she making them so big and magnetic on purpose? How was she doing that? Was this a gentlemen-and-ladies thing?

And then somehow she answered my question. "I mean, not in like a 'what would a gentleman do' way," she said, leaning forward, setting aside her glass. "Like really. If *I*, me, wanted to kiss *you*—just you—what about that? Would that be good?"

"Why would you?" I asked, before I could stop myself.

Her face scrunched up at the question. She was close now, and I could see how her teeth pulled at her lower lip as she thought. "Like why would I want to? Really? I mean, first of all, you're pretty cute. I mean actually you're hot. Really hot. I think so, anyway. But I guess what's more important is that I feel really connected to you. I feel like you don't have to be a gentleman. You're a lot more interesting just as you are."

I tried clearing my throat, but my head was still buzzing. "For the record, Mel, I think you're really attractive too. And interesting. Never mind all the stuff about the café and whatever. I—"

I'm honestly not exactly sure what I intended to say. Every thought flew out of my head when she leaned forward and kissed me.

She just kissed me briefly at first, leaning over from her spot on the couch. She pulled back almost immediately.

"Oops, sorry," she said, a bit breathlessly. "I just realized I didn't actually wait for your answer. To my question. I mean, I asked you if it was fine if I kissed you and you never actually *said* it was but I kind of figured—"

"My answer is yes," I told her, pulling her closer. I just remember hearing her laugh for one brief second before we were kissing again.

Mel had her hands on my shoulders, and then around my neck, and then somehow she was in my lap. I remember the sharp pain in my wrist because I couldn't hold her the way I wanted to, but I must not have made any sound, because she didn't stop. Her hair smelled exactly the way it always did and of course we both tasted like wine but on top of that there was this warmth and sweetness, like she was pulling me into some kind of spell. If it had been actual magic, I would have been a complete goner. As it was, I barely remembered to hold myself back and breathe eventually.

"This'd probably be better if I could use both my hands," I remember mumbling to her apologetically.

But of course, she chuckled. Her face was still so close to mine, her arms entwined around my neck. "It's fine. I think it's really good, actually. But I'm probably out of practice. I haven't—haven't really kissed anyone since . . . well, since before my accident."

"I haven't since before I came here," I admitted without thinking. What time was there for thinking? I don't think I had any unoccupied brain space left.

"Really?" Mel sounded surprised, but she kept her head close to mine, so it wasn't alarming or anything. Kind of cute, in fact, that she thought I should be out breaking hearts or something.

Of course, the last thing on my mind was to tell her the *reason* I hadn't been going around dating or kissing people. But she was still curled up around me, and I could feel her breathing, and it was exciting but also so *comfortable.* That's what I remember most. I felt so free, even though I was stuck on a couch with a bad leg and a bad arm to boot. I probably would have told her anything she wanted to know. Even though that's what I was most afraid of doing, because giving her answers might drive her away. But even though I knew that—I *always* knew that, with Mel—somehow in that moment, fear didn't feel real.

So, like I said. I probably would have told her anything. But she never got to ask. At that moment, there was a loud, insistent knock on the door, and Mel jumped out of my lap like she was the picture of innocence and I was the epitome of guilt.

## Thirteen

*Any Press . . .*

Mel

Kissing Ryuko was probably a bad idea.

I mean, it definitely was a bad idea, right? Because he was just into me in order to save his own hide from some silly holiday auction. It was all a farce. And hadn't that been exactly what I hated about big city life before my accident finally brought things into perspective for me?

I didn't need a fairy godmother to answer that. The answer was *yes*.

But even though I *knew* that, because I kept reminding myself of it—when I remembered to, which was only times when I *wasn't* looking at him, or laughing at something he'd said, or sitting in his lap—anyway, I *knew* that, but even so, it didn't *feel* like it. Actually that afternoon with Ryuko felt really good. It felt so real, in a way that so much of my life *hadn't* up to that point. The kind of real that I'd been chasing ever since my brush with death. The whole reason I'd moved to Belville and decided to start throwing myself into life in the first place. Nothing about it felt like a farce.

But that was probably just the wine . . .

At least, on *his* side, I knew it must be just the wine. On my side—well, let's just say I was feeling pretty messy. My head, my heart, my stomach full of alcohol—nothing was agreeing very much on anything.

So I stood there, embarrassed by my own foolishness, feeling pulled in five different directions, trying not to let Sakura on to the fact that I'd just totally been coming on to her brother.

*Does she know? What does he think? Have I eaten anything recently?*

"Oh, hi," Sakura said, taking in the scene. "We just finished up at the café and I wanted to come check on the patient. I tried knocking, but no one answered, and I couldn't hear anything, and then wouldn't you know—the door was open."

I was pretty sure I always locked my doors. It was a big city habit. But I was also pretty sure that my iron locks wouldn't keep out a worried shadow witch.

"Looks like everything's . . . fine?" Sakura continued, looking at me with her head to one side. "Mel, why do you look like you just kicked a puppy?"

And just like that, I was sober. *She knows.*

I stammered and tried to come up with something to say, but Sakura's gaze swept down over the table and she noticed our glasses. Her mouth fell open. "Ryu, were you *drinking?*"

"Is that bad?" I asked, catching the tone in her voice, looking at him.

"I haven't since I moved here," he told me, like it was no big deal. Now *my* mouth was wide open, too. I'd had no idea! "And yes, Saki, we had some wine. It's not a big deal. Technically I promised you I wouldn't drink *without friends,* anyway. It's not like I'm going to find myself in this situation again."

This situation? What did he mean? Conscripted by his sister into an auction he didn't like and facing the prospect of a fake romance or a forced date and also dealing with bruises and mended bones from a construction-related injury at the café where said auction would take place? Or dealing with my sloppy advances?

Two guesses which option I immediately decided *must* be true.

"I—I had no idea," I finally managed, as Sakura looked back at me. "I'm so sorry."

"You don't have anything to be sorry for," Ryuko growled.

"That's right, Mel. You should have told her," Sakura said, focusing on her brother. "The deal was *friends who know,* so they can look after you!"

"I was just trying to help," I reminded the room at large. In case there *were* any fairy godmothers listening. All the warm fuzzies from kissing Ryuko were long gone. I felt *awful.*

"I've been fine for years, and I'll *be* fine. It's more about the situation I'm in than anything else," Ryuko was arguing.

"*None* of this would have happened if you could just communicate," Sakura was arguing right back.

"What do you mean, none?" I asked, hopelessly out of the loop.

"That's rich from the girl who won't ask for help until she wants you to go on a cursed *stage* and sell yourself for a made-up event," Ryuko shot back, clearly ignoring me.

I looked at Sakura. I hadn't realized she had trouble asking for help.

"You've been helping with the café from day one. And that isn't the point here," Sakura insisted, black sparkles of magic flaring around her bright white hair as her temper snapped. "Trent told me everything. You're totally out of control!"

"It was *my* idea. And it was only a few glasses of wine," I said meekly. Unfortunately for me, the siblings had apparently hit a stopping point in their fight. My words met with silence, and they both stared at me.

Sakura fumed for another minute before saying, "I'm too worked up to have this conversation right now. I'm leaving. Trent told me you have to stay put for at least a day, Ryu. So you stay *put*!"

She stormed out. And when Ryuko didn't get up to follow in her wake—because honestly, how could he, with his injured leg?—I turned to him awkwardly.

"Um . . ." I twisted my hands, trying to unravel all the things I'd heard and the things I was afraid of.

"I'll go to Trent's," Ryuko muttered.

"You don't—you really don't have to. You're not supposed to. Remember? That's even farther than your house would be. That's definitely not staying put. You can stay here," I said.

He grimaced. "I'm not a charity case."

"Of course not. You're an injured—" I flailed, unable to come up with the right noun. *Friend? Partner in crime? Lover? Why, oh why, do I want that last one to be true?* He was staring at me, so I finally squeaked out, "Guest."

Anger sparked in his eyes and for a moment, I could see how he and Sakura *had* grown up together. But unlike her, he stowed his anger away, turning to face the wall and grinding out, "I guess I'll sleep on the couch then, *if you insist.*"

"I do insist," I said, vaguely wondering when we'd started fighting. Was it about the wine? "I'm—um—I'm really sorry about all this. I never should have. I just had no idea. I'm so, so sorry—I didn't mean to cause any trouble. I was just trying to be . . ." Words failed me, again, and this time he refused to look at me at all. "Well, anyway, I'll—um—I'll—we should eat something. I'll get something. Then I'll get some blankets and—I mean, you can stay here as long as you like. You know where everything is, I guess, I mean I know we haven't exactly done a tour, but it's such a small house you can probably see all the rooms from here . . . Anyway, right. Food. I'll go get that."

I escaped to the kitchen like a dying fish thrown back into cool, quiet water. At least alone, there was no one staring at me—or staring at anything *other* than me. That feeling of being invisible haunted me to my core. *Definitely better,* I decided, *to give him some space.*

But was it? I couldn't shake my feeling of guilt. I scrounged up food and brought some into the living room for him, but he didn't say anything—and I didn't either. In fact, after that I pretty much ran away and ate my dinner outside. It was cold, and dark, and I wasn't *trying* to be melodramatic, I just . . . couldn't quite believe everything that had happened.

Not the fact that he hadn't told me about not drinking, not the fact that Saki was having problems getting the café together, not the fact that now I had an invalid on my couch. Not the fact that I'd kissed him.

Not the fact that for a moment, he'd seemed happy about it. In fact, the more I thought, the more I believed that one least of all.

A night's sleep didn't help much, either. I tossed and turned and eventually got up and left before dawn, which was my routine anyway, but it felt so strange and foreign now. I did leave things out for Ryuko, because even if he was mad at me he was still in recovery, and besides—I wasn't quite sure if I was mad at him or not. I mean, obviously what Saki had said about him being more communicative was true. I did wish he had told me more. But—the way I saw it, that wasn't exactly a reason to be *mad*. Frustrated and disappointed, maybe, but it wasn't like I'd asked him a question and he'd lied.

Anyway, suffice it to say, I was pretty much a zombie at work that day. If Abi tried to talk to me, I'm not sure I even said a word in response. In the morning I had a pretty intense headache, of course—I don't actually drink all that often, and not sleeping on top of that hadn't helped. By the afternoon the fog was starting to clear, but I still felt miserable somehow. I wasn't sure whether to go back to the café or not. Sakura was obviously mad at her brother—was she mad at me too? And with him so mad at me, the whole charade was definitely off.

*Charade.* The word stung.

To distract myself, I tried to take a little more interest in my route. It was newspaper day, which meant I picked up a weekly edition of the local paper from Leo, a one-woman reporter and editor and printer. I then delivered it to all the businesses along the Square during my afternoon rounds. Many copies went to Lavender's Tavern, of course, so I stopped there first. By the end of the round, I usually had a paper to keep to myself. I think Leo printed extras on purpose, but I *had* made a point of setting up a subscription when I came to town. After all, what better way to get to know a small community than by reading its weekly news? And to add to that, my father might have disowned me if I didn't value the local paper. In fact, I knew that my parents had a copy of Belville's news delivered to their home in New Dale by a special magical express every week. Normally it was a savored, quiet moment, reading the paper in the Square at the end of my day.

But today I didn't make it all the way through my route before I found myself reading an article, flabbergasted. It was a headline below the fold on the front page that had caught my eye.

*True Love Sparked by Saint Valentine's Feast at Pomegranate Café?*

At first I was just idly curious. I had a few steps to go until my next stop, and I was feeling so mixed up that honestly I had forgotten the name of Sakura's café. But then I noticed the little illustration that went beside the article.

It was a drawing of *me.* Holding up a heart mobile with none other than the man I'd kissed last night, who subsequently wanted nothing whatsoever to do with me.

So then of course I stopped walking that very minute, and I had to read the whole thing.

*Pomegranate's opening is shaping up to be the event of the season, if not the year!*

*Owner Sakura, 26, plans on hosting a themed dinner on Saint Valentine's Day. Price of admission includes lovers' pasta, wine, delectable baked goods, and most unique of all—access to the special auction.*

*"We've got a variety of gift baskets and presents to auction off,"* Sakura says, *"but the real prize of the evening is a date with Ryuko."*

*Ryuko, 31, is a familiar—and elusive—face around town. No doubt the bidder who wins a free dinner with him would be rewarded with an incomparable look behind the scenes of that handsome glower! However, bidders looking for true love may be disappointed. It seems that something's blooming between event coordinator Mel and the bachelor in question. Mel, 32, recently settled in town and working as the new postmaster, was not available for comment. Word on the streets is that the couple works well together, and one look at the decorations in the Pomegranate proves this to be true. One anonymous source even mentioned late-night visits . . . planning sessions for the auction, perhaps?*

I dropped my stack of newspapers on the ground.

This is when I *really* needed some fairy godmother guidance.

Because if Ryuko didn't kill me, then my mother definitely would.

## Fourteen

# Code (Valentine's) Red

Ryuko

I f I didn't like Mel so much, then none of this would have been a problem. Sakura taking on too much for herself to handle and then berating me about not communicating wasn't anything new. Being injured was honestly nothing, especially since Trent had sped the healing along. But the way Mel had leapt away from me . . . I hated that. I hated any thought of losing her.

Which was foolish, because she wasn't mine. In what world would an ex-criminal be remotely good enough for her? Only in Saki's make-believe romance world could we even have crossed paths.

And believe me, as I lay on Mel's couch all morning alone, I had time to think up some pretty choice words for Saki.

It was probably a good thing that around lunchtime, I was no longer alone.

"Hey," Trent called from the front door, before letting himself in. In his battered jeans and faded t-shirt, he was the least intimidating home intruder possible. His skin was so pale it practically glowed in the gloom, and his dark chin-length hair was a mess. Aside from Priya and Red, Trent was my one long-standing friend in town. I probably should have been happy to see him. Instead I just scowled from my spot on the couch.

"Yeah, that's about what I expected," he observed with a lopsided grin. He sat on Mel's armchair like a grasshopper, folded and gangly. "Saki told me everything that happened."

I returned to glaring at the ceiling. Trent was a good guy, and a really good Witch. Even though he was probably five or six years younger than me, about Sakura's age, he'd always been steady. That was, until Saki showed up in town. I still hadn't decided how I felt about him being so into my baby sister.

"I figured I better stop by and see how the healing's going," Trent continued casually. "You should have seen it last night. Saki made me magic everything back into place, and had Dusty test it all about five times at least. I haven't done so much levitation since Witch school. I was totally wiped out this morning. But I was thinking, depending on how well you're knitting up, I could try to give healing you another turn."

This merited a glance. I have no magic, but I knew how important it was for witches to rest and recharge before doing more spells. Saki was always going on about "energy" and "balance." If Trent was offering to try healing me again, he must feel pretty bad about the whole thing.

Not to mention if he healed me all the way, I'd be able to get up and give Saki a piece of my mind.

"Hold up, though," Trent said, holding up his hands. He must have read the look on my face. "I'm not here to add fuel to any fires. I heal you, we go out to the tavern and have a massive lunch. That's the deal. Sound good?"

If Trent thought lunch would be enough to calm my frustration, he had another think coming. But more likely the lunch was for his own sake. The bags under his eyes proved that he probably wasn't in the best condition to try healing again already. But if he was offering . . .

"Fine," I said, shifting to sit upright. "Deal."

"Cool." Trent nodded and crossed over to sit on the floor next to my bad ankle. "Leg first, right?"

"Sure," I agreed. "The worst thing is not being able to walk on my own."

"Makes sense." Trent was quiet for a moment, his magic glowing purple as he scanned the injury and did whatever healing Witches do. All I know about magic, I learned from Sakura. And since Saki's a rogue witch, not an official town Witch or anything, she never had to learn all the spells and specialties that Trent knows.

The bottom line is, I just picked a spot on Mel's carpet and focused on that. I did my best to ignore the tingling and cramps and jolts that came from the magic. The carpet was deep, a sort of faded green color. Mel had mentioned that the cottage belonged to her grandmother. That was pretty obvious from the outdated decorating. *The place could definitely use some updates,* I decided. A new door and lock, for one. Probably a new faucet—I'd listened to the kitchen sink dripping all night. Maybe pull up the carpet and take a look at the wood floors beneath. Dusty would know what to do about that.

"Okay," Trent announced. He was breathing heavily, and he pushed his hair out of his face with a shaky hand. But he grinned as he looked up. "I think that did it. You might as well try putting some weight on it now, and see how it does. Just slowly, though," he added, as I started to stand up.

But I'd had enough of being helpless on a couch. I was going to stand no matter *how* it felt.

That said—it didn't feel too bad. When Trent slid onto the couch and tilted his head, curious, I said honestly, "It's sore, but it's nothing compared to what it was."

"Perfect." Trent nodded, then tipped his head back, resting against the cushions. He kept talking to the ceiling. "I'm like ninety-nine percent sure I got all the damage to the bone cleared up, so you shouldn't be in any danger of making it worse. Keep going easy on it, obviously, but at this point it's just the muscles taking some time to get back to normal."

"Yeah, no problem." I knew that for as casual as Trent might sound, he'd probably done a better job than half the doctors in Brass could have done. That was just how he was. And besides, I could feel how much more solid my leg felt. "Thanks."

"Thank me by taking care of it," Trent said, tugging at my arm to get me to sit back down. As I did, he added, "I'd take a look at your wrist if I could, but I don't think I could do any good for it even if you threatened to kill me. I'm just glad the ankle thing worked."

"Don't worry about it," I told him. "You've done enough."

"Thanks. Be sure and tell your sister that, will you?" Trent slid his gaze to me, just out of the corner of his eye, and then he grinned again. "Not that it'd do any good. Maybe never mind on that. She'll come around on her own eventually."

I snorted. "Glad to see *you* have faith."

"Yeah, I imagine you aren't feeling too peachy about romance just about now." With an effort, Trent sat up and met my eye. "Listen, if there's anything I can do, just let me know. I know the last thing you want now is advice from someone like me."

"I don't need advice about Sakura," I said, confused.

"I know that. I meant advice about Mel," Trent said, elbowing me in a friendly way.

"What did you hear about me and Mel?"

"Just that you were staying here." He spoke blithely as he stood and looked around. "Most of it I just put together from what I saw yesterday and a few things Saki said about how you all got fed up last night. Not that I know Mel very well. She usually does the town route with the mail, right? I think someone else does the outer houses and my Hut."

This was quickly going to places I didn't want to talk about. I stood abruptly. "I owe you lunch, right?"

"Something like that. I'm starving," Trent said, as agreeable as ever. "Think we'll see her while we're in town?"

"See who?" Mel's front door flew open as Saki came in unexpectedly, her arms full of steaming mugs and bags of pastries. She saw me and her eyes narrowed. "What are you doing standing up?"

"He's fine," Trent said hastily. "I did another round of healing. He still has to go easy on it, but most of the work is done. We were going to go get lunch at the tavern. Want to come?"

"Lunch? It's already tea time," Saki said, moving to put her things on the table. Apparently she hadn't warmed up to Trent just yet. "Who did you want to see?"

She looked at me as she said it. I ground my teeth.

"Mel," Trent said eventually, sticking his hands in his pockets.

Saki tilted her head. "I thought she'd left work early and

come back here?"

That made no sense. But as I looked down, I saw that Sakura had brought three cups from the café. And since she obviously hadn't expected Trent, she really must have thought Mel was at home. "Why would you think that?" I asked, alarms ringing at the back of my mind.

"Because she never came by for the end of her afternoon round," Saki said, her face falling as she straightened up. "I checked at Red's and Gloria's, but they hadn't seen her. Someone else brought the paper round. And—the paper had an article in it about her . . . and *you,* Ryu."

If I'd've gritted my teeth any harder, they would've been sand.

"We could trace her," Trent suggested.

"*You* don't have enough magic left to pop a bubble," Sakura told him pointedly.

I was already moving to the door. I knew exactly where to look.

## Fifteen

# *Magic is Better Than Boats?*

## Mel

I have to admit, I did think about chucking Leo's papers straight into the lake.

But of course, the fish probably wouldn't have appreciated that, and knowing my luck, some magical lake creature probably would have appeared to take its revenge. Although really, that might not have been such a bad thing. I might have better luck with a lake creature than with Sakura and my mother . . . and Ryuko.

And my feelings.

That's actually why I took the rest of the afternoon off. Not because of the paper exactly, but just because I knew I had a lot of processing to do—and I also didn't feel up to looking anyone in the face. Fortunately, the ever-dependable Katia was happy to take up the slack. I didn't even head home, because I knew Ryuko would still be there. Instead, I took off toward the boathouse, still in my uniform and everything.

Paddling helps me clear my mind. Out on a lake or river, watching the birds along the shore and the fish under the waves, seeing the wind ripple the water and listening to the movement all around, I really feel like I am part of *life*. I'm not sure if that makes any sense, especially to people who prefer to stay on dry land. But it's something I've always loved, ever since I was a kid. Of course, it wasn't a very lady-like habit, so my parents had never been too pleased about it. But now that I was an adult and living on my own in a new town, I'd devoted myself to the sport.

I was pretty good, in my own way, but it's not like I was a champion rower or anything. I was just out paddling around in an old canoe, really. I never went too far from shore. Just going back and forth was enough, skirting the coastline, feeling that chilly spring breeze and trying to get all of everyone *else*'s opinions out of my head. *How do I feel about all this?*

By the fourth lap, I was starting to feel calm enough to where I might actually be able to think straight. By the fifth lap, I was considering courses of action. I could give up and leave Belville . . . or maybe just leave for a little while? No. Those were admitting defeat, something I had no interest in doing. I could . . . talk to someone? That sounded terrifying, but I probably *ought* to, at least to Sakura . . .

Funnily enough, just as I was thinking of the shadow witch, I noticed a small clump of figures waving from the dock.

One was short and wearing vibrant red, visible even at a distance. One was gangly and hanging back a bit. And the final one was tall, and it made my heart skip a beat.

So, I recognized them, of course. But I didn't row toward them. After all, my canoe was already pointed in the opposite direction, and I still wasn't a very slick navigator. And besides, what could they have to say to me? How could they have found me? It was probably all a coincidence, and they were just waving at each other.

From a few feet away.

Okay, maybe that didn't make sense. I knew that at the time, and honestly I probably *would* have turned around and headed in, out of curiosity—or guilt. But just as I was getting the prow of the canoe to come around, and I was parallel with the dock, I looked over my shoulder and noticed that someone *else* was now on the lake.

Two someones.

I watched with deep misgivings as Ryuko and Sakura's rowboat lurched toward me.

"You really don't have to do that," I called, as they came within hearing range. "I'll come in."

"Like heck you will," Ryuko called back, over his shoulder. He had one oar, and Sakura appeared to have wrestled the other away from him, because she was rowing at an awkward angle that definitely wasn't helping their boat. "You saw the article, didn't you?"

"I did," I confirmed, still yelling to be heard over their splashing. "But it's not like I was going to stay out on the lake forever."

Ryuko snorted, and it sounded an awful lot like, "*Says the woman who's always trying to run away!*"

"Hey!" I protested, my shame and confusion turning quickly into offended pride. "You're just jealous you can't run, because you have a bad leg!"

"I'm fine now. Trent fixed me," he shouted back.

"He's not fine!" Sakura interjected, sounding breathless. "Can we have this conversation on dry land, please?"

"*You* can go back. You weren't invited in the first place," Ryuko told her.

"Can we all just be nice?" I called, exasperated.

But in my exasperation I'd failed to account for something, and that something was the speed with which Ryuko was rowing. Even though their progress was haphazard and uneven, it was still *progress*. And since I hadn't moved, they were progressing right for me.

A second after I noticed this and started to panic, it was too late. Ryuko and Sakura's boat crashed into mine. I didn't even have time to think before I went tumbling over the side away from them, into the frigid water.

And when I came back up, I wasn't the only one in the lake.

"You shouldn't be here," I yelled at Ryuko, spitting water. We both clung to the edge of my empty canoe. *His* boat was still perfectly fine, bobbing nearby, and hardly upset, since it had rammed me head-on.

"I came in for *you*," he spat back. "You're welcome."

"So now we're *both* freezing? Why should I be grateful about that?"

"You should be grateful I don't go around making as big a deal out of things as you do!"

"How is jumping in after me, when I'm perfectly fine on my own, not making a big deal of things?"

I thought this was a very good point, and when Ryuko didn't answer at first, I felt triumphant. But then I realized that we were both hanging in the air, held aloft by black tendrils of magic.

"*Neither* of you are fine!" Sakura shouted at us. She had her hands uplifted and spread as she worked the spell that had plucked us from the lake. "You're both going straight to Trent's to get treated for hypothermia, and so help me goddess, if you step out of line one more time I'm putting a twenty-four hour watch on you both!"

I might have argued—and I was sure *Ryuko* would have argued—but now that we were exposed to the wind, I realized how cold it really was. The sun was already setting. My teeth chattered too rapidly for me to form words.

The next hour was a blur. Much as I wanted to stay on my own—okay, so maybe Ryuko was a *little* right about me running away—there was no way I could have properly cared for myself. Somehow—probably sheer force of will—Sakura got us both to Trent's official witchy residence, called "the Hut," which wasn't too far from the lake. There, Trent took over, making us change into dry pajamas and sit by the fire while he made herbal teas and foot baths. He must have grumbled quite a bit about food, I think—whether for us or for him, I wasn't sure—because at some point Sakura disappeared, promising to get dinner and more hot drinks.

"We're fine," Ryuko growled after she'd left.

"Yeah," said Trent dismissively. He hovered over where we sat in two mismatched wooden chairs, mere inches from the blazing hearth. "That didn't work on Saki, and it won't work on me either. Just because I'm not scary when I'm mad doesn't mean I'm a pushover."

The way he said it made me laugh. But when I did, Ryuko glanced sideways at me, like somehow I was taking sides against him.

Well, I'd had enough. I frowned back. "What? Stop looking at me like that. None of this is my fault. You didn't have to come out onto the lake."

"And you didn't have to try to go and use your injured arm, either," Trent added to Ryuko. "You know I'm all tapped out, healing-wise. At this point you'll probably end up with your wrist fractured again, and pneumonia on top of that."

"Wait—that was a joke, right?" I asked, but Trent was already running back down to his cellar, where apparently he kept all kinds of herbs for just this sort of occasion. I looked back at Ryuko. "Tell me that was a joke?"

His dark green eyes seemed to waver for a minute as he looked at me. But then he just glared at the fire, and I decided that anything I might've seen was just reflections of the dancing flames. "I didn't fracture it," he muttered unhelpfully.

"Oh, gods and goddesses." I slumped in my chair as the reality of the situation set in. "Why doesn't this town have a proper doctor?"

"Because it's the sticks," Ryuko said. "You didn't have to move here."

"I don't even know what we're fighting about any more," I said, my exasperation coming back in a wave. "Can we please just call a truce?"

"Yeah, do that, at least while you're in my house," Trent said as he reappeared. "It's too small in here for fighting. I got some more elderberry, to help ward off fever. And I was kinda kidding," he added, smiling kindly at me as he sat down beside us and started throwing dried leaves into the fire and into the hot baths for our feet. "It's not as bad as all that. And if it *does* turn out bad, then after I get some food—finally—and some sleep, I should be able to reverse the damage."

"You must be a really good healer," I said, calming down a little as I watched him work. Back in New Dale I'd seen both doctors and magical healers, and while some were as ambitious as Trent seemed to be, most had to scale back their efforts to enable them to treat many different patients.

Trent shrugged bashfully. "In school I always thought it was kinda boring, but now that I see how useful it is in town, I kinda like it."

"He's gotten really good," Ryuko said firmly, and unexpectedly. He sat up, but still avoided my gaze. "This'll all blow over."

"Of course it will," Trent agreed. "No lasting harm done."

This was reassuring, at least. As Trent sat back, poking at the fire, I took a sip of my tea. Between the steaming mug, the smoking fire, and the borrowed flannel pajamas and blanket around my shoulders, I was starting to forget what being cold had ever felt like in the first place. And the tension was finally easing from my shoulders a bit.

"Why were you all out at the dock?" I asked, impulsively.

Trent looked at Ryuko, and when he didn't say anything, explained, "I was just following Ryuko and Saki. I'd stopped by your place to check on him. Hope you don't mind, by the way."

"No, that's fine," I assured him, thinking *well, Belville may not have a proper doctor, but at least the local healer makes house calls.* It was clear that Trent cared about *both* Sakura and Ryuko, and that made me like him all the more. Anyone who could care about Ryuko had to be a determined soul.

"Cool. So, while we were there talking, Sakura came by and mentioned how no one'd seen you in a while. Then she let it slip about the paper . . ." Again, Trent glanced at Ryuko. Again, Ryuko said nothing. "It, ah, seemed like maybe the article might have made you upset."

"It did," I agreed. Having Trent there made the words easier to say. "This whole day has been kind of a mess, in my opinion. But I really wasn't running away or anything."

*Well, I was considering how to live here without ever encountering Sakura or Ryuko again, but does that really count?*

"Yeah, no, I don't think we actually thought that," Trent said, as the voice of reason. "I think maybe . . . well, I think Saki feels bad about it, to tell you the truth. I don't think any of this has gone how she planned."

"Are you saying you came down to the docks to apologize?" I asked slowly.

"Well, I think that's what Saki had in mind. That's just me thinking that, though. She didn't actually tell me that. As for Ryuko . . ." Trent glanced at his friend once more, and Ryuko finally looked over at him. An unspoken hint seemed to pass between them, because Trent abruptly stood. "I'm going to go see about more feverfew for another round of tea."

In his wake, I stared at Ryuko. And, finally, Ryuko lifted his gaze to me.

"I didn't know anything about it," he said, his voice a little raspy.

"I know. I mean, I figured you didn't," I said at once, leaning in despite myself. "It really doesn't seem like your style."

The corner of his mouth crooked up. "Neither is jumping into lakes after ladies."

"But that, you did," I said, smiling. "And I probably shouldn't have given you such a hard time for it. Your heart was obviously in the right place. Honestly, I probably owe *you* an apology for the way I reacted."

Ryuko looked surprised, whether by the apology or something else, I couldn't say. He hesitated. After a moment, he said, "Listen, Mel . . . Sakura's been a real pain, and I don't agree with some of the things she's done. But just because I'm mad at her doesn't mean I'm mad at you. You know that, right?"

Now *I* was surprised, and it was because of the gentleness in his voice. I hadn't really seen that side of him before, not fully. And I hadn't expected him to make the distinction. "Well, I—I do get that," I said, a little uncertain. "But I thought—last night, I thought you might be mad at me specifically."

His brows knitted together. "Why? We already went over how you had no idea about the wine. That was my choice."

"Of course, that's totally up to you," I agreed hastily. "That's not really what I meant.  I was thinking more because of—well—I know this whole situation has been something you didn't want, necessarily, and I wasn't trying to make it harder or anything, or trying to complicate things.  I wasn't sure if you—maybe you thought I—got too close."

"Too close?" His eyes widened.

"Right.  By kissing you," I said in a rush.  "I know it's not anything you thought should happen, probably. I didn't mean to make you uncomfortable.  I'm really not trying to take advantage of you or anything, I swear. I just—well—I mean I actually did have a really good time with you, and I know we argue a lot too, and all, but—"

Fortunately, as I groped for words in the silence, both willing myself to say and *not* to say *I like you*, I heard footsteps outside. My mouth clamped shut at once. *Salvation!*

"Dinner!" Sakura called, as she opened the front door. Her gaze swept over us by the fire, and I couldn't help but think of the night before. My cheeks flushed.

Apparently, though, Saki was preoccupied. "Where is Trent?

Don't tell me he left you two alone!"

And very, very faintly, so that only I could hear, and even then I doubted I heard it at all, Ryuko murmured, "Gods forbid *you* do the same."

## Sixteen

## Love and Murder

Ryuko

I'd thought Mel found me embarrassing. Or off-putting. Or annoying, at the very least. But for a moment back there, it'd sounded like she might like me. The way her voice had gone all breathy and her eyes had gone soft definitely had me thinking about how much I liked her. Even though I shouldn't.

And so naturally, when we were about to clear up the whole ridiculous mess, Saki walked in.

If I'd been mad at my little sister before, I could have killed her in that moment. Luckily for her, Trent popped his head up through the floor. I owed Trent, for healing me and for taking care of Mel. I couldn't murder the girl he had a crush on right in front of him.

So instead, I went back to staring at the fire. And I stayed that way through most of the night. Sakura had brought soup and fresh bread from the tavern, which did help my mood a little. But it didn't help that pit in my stomach.

What had Mel been about to say? Did she really like me after all? And if she did—how in Beyond was I going to tell her about myself? Who I used to be? And while we were on that topic, what did I really have to offer her, anyway? I worked part time, lived in a ratty apartment with two roommates, and had no real prospects.

Not surprisingly, that line of thought didn't have me feeling very cheery. And when Sakura insisted that we all stay over, for a brief moment I didn't mind the idea. I hoped to get another chance to talk to Mel. But I should have known better. With Trent and Saki hovering, watching us for any signs of bronchitis or whatever, we never had a moment to spare. And after all the chaos—and not sleeping the night before—I ended up sleeping a lot more than I expected.

When I woke up the next morning, Mel was already long gone. And since it was the day before the big auction, Sakura was in full go-mode.

The moment Trent wrapped up my wrist and declared that I was in full health, we were on the move. Sure, I was angry still, but I'd already taken off work to help with the auction and I wasn't going to leave Saki hanging. I did all the moving and carpentry and taste-testing required of me, I just did it with poor grace. Which, I realized, wasn't much of a change from usual. I also realized it was a total drag. Despite the annoyance of it all, the first days of prep had been much more fun. Maybe Mel with her bright public face was onto something.

But Mel, having an actual job and all, wasn't there for most of the day. Then as soon as the afternoon hit and she was due to show up, Sakura grabbed my arm and literally dragged me out into the decrepit garage behind the café.

"Do you want to undo all your boyfriend's work?" I asked, jerking my hand away from her.

"He isn't my boyfriend. Do you know that's the longest sentence you've said to me all day?" she shot back as she closed the door behind us. Seeing as it was just a bunch of old planks held together by dust, it still let in plenty of light. And that was good, since the building had no lights of its own. It was basically a barn.

It was also freezing, and full of junk, and *exactly* how my mind felt on the inside. I crossed my arms and glared. "You don't want to hear what I have to say to you."

"Yes I do," Sakura retorted. "You know me. I'm all about facing issues head-on. Unless I'm so mad at you I can't see straight, or so busy with the café that I don't have time for yelling."

"But now suddenly you *do* have time?" I asked, raising an eyebrow.

"Now that Mel is going to show up and take over and I don't want you being a growly bear at her, yes, I have time," Sakura said, perching on a stack of boxes. "Come on, let's have it."

I leaned back against a pile of rusty old cartwheels. Just my luck and the whole thing would collapse. But the truth was, my injured ankle still hurt a bit. Not that I'd ever say that aloud. "I don't know what to say to you."

"Then I'll start." As usual, Sakura sounded entirely too cheerful. "Ryu, you could have been seriously hurt the other day. And yesterday at the lake, too."

"You're mad at me for accidentally falling over a weak banister?"

"No, I was *worried*. Which I admit, came out as pretty much the same thing, because I've also been so frustrated with you," she said. "Look, Ryu, I know you weren't happy about this from the beginning. But you've been so weird about it lately. It's like you're not focusing. I know you. I know how careful you are. The Ryuko I grew up with would never fall over a banister. What are you doing?"

"What do you mean, what am I doing? I'm doing what you said."

"No, you're not. *I* said to help me put on an auction, and to act like you have a crush on our event planner. Instead, you're falling over things, jumping into lakes, drinking *wine*, refusing to talk to anyone, and obviously driving poor Mel to distraction. That's like five different things at least."

"You think I'm driving Mel to distraction?" I shifted. "In a good way or a bad one?"

"Focus, please! This is exactly what I'm talking about," Sakura complained.

"What you said to do was doomed from the start," I said, and it felt good to finally get it off my chest. "It was a terrible idea and I never should have agreed. I'm not good enough for Emmelayne de Foret, Saki."

"First of all, of course you are, you're good enough for anyone, because love isn't something you're 'good enough' for," she retorted. "And second—I didn't say to *actually* fall in love, so I didn't think it would matter."

"Don't lie," I growled. "I know what you've been up to. You've been playing matchmaker from the start."

Sakura's eyes widened for a moment. Then she grinned.

"Well, I won't say I didn't think about it," she admitted. "But you're the one who started it."

"What's that supposed to mean?"

"Oh, come on, Ryu," she cried. "You two obviously have chemistry. A spark. You have since the very first morning we all spoke. Don't you feel it? Or are you so wrapped up in waiting for someone to tell you that you *get* to start over that you won't let yourself see what's right in front of you?"

For a long moment, I was silent. The blow was a hard one, but I knew it was true. As a shadow witch accustomed to exploring her own dark emotions, Sakura rarely pulled her punches. But she was also rarely wrong. Eventually I said, gruffly, "The very first morning we all spoke, we didn't have *chemistry*. I was mad at her for stressing out my already-stressed little sister."

Sakura snorted. "More like mad you didn't have a reason to kiss her right there on the sidewalk." She walked over and poked my shoulder, leaning against the wheels next to me. "You can't fool me. I have a sense for these things."

"Yeah. I know." I sighed. Still refusing to look at her, I added, "But if you're gonna put your powers to good use, or whatever, you've got to get better about your matchmaking. A magitech steamroller is more subtle than you."

Sakura giggled. "It's just because you're my brother. I just really need you to stop being so foolish and be *happy* already."

"I'd be a lot happier if someone didn't keep interrupting Mel before she can admit she likes me," I said, still disgruntled.

"Is that what you two were talking about last night?" Sakura tilted her head, clearly turning this over in her mind for a moment before saying, "Well, I *am* sorry about that. And I still have to apologize to her properly, too. But I'm sure that if she does really like you, that holds just as true today as it did yesterday. It's not like news like that goes bad. And besides," she added, warming to her theme, "have you considered that *you* could just go ahead and admit that you like *her* first?"

"I probably ought to. I ought to just tell her the first moment I see her, before you get a chance to interrupt," I said grumpily. But as appealing as the thought was, it was terrifying too. I shrugged it off even as Saki nodded enthusiastically. "I'm not doing that."

"Well, why not?" she needled.

I knew she'd get it out of me eventually. Staring up at the rafters, I admitted, "I haven't told her anything, Saki. About where we came from. Who I used to be. Getting caught and sentenced to a year of service, for gods' sakes."

"So? She's not a time traveler. She likes you now, not then."

"She's basically a lady," I protested. "She can't be seen going around with someone like me."

"Did you *see* her yesterday in her goofy uniform on a boat in storm weather?" Sakura snorted, but it was clear she was coming from a place of affection. She really did like Mel. How could anyone *not* like Mel? "It's clear she doesn't care what people see," Saki added. "Remember, she came here for a new start too. Just like you. Why won't you let her have one? Why won't you let yourself? You're getting so caught up on your 'should not's and 'ought to's. When are you going to let go of them, and just let yourself *live*?"

I knew without looking down what the look on Sakura's face would be. Sisterly concern and a little bit of exasperation. We'd been having this conversation ever since she'd come to Belville and realized how I was living.

Or, more accurately, not living at all.

In fact, Sakura's list of the things I'd been doing since I met

Mel—falling, jumping, making silly hearts—it all sounded a lot more like living than anything else I'd ever done.

And for the first time in the *many* that Sakura had asked me why I wasn't letting myself live, I felt something inside me thaw. *A new start.* That was exactly what Mel wanted. What she deserved. What she'd made for herself, for gods' sakes.

"She really likes event planning," I said, quietly. "More than she expected. She said as much to me the other day while we were making all your cursed hearts."

"I think it's pretty clear she also really likes talking to you," Sakura said. But her voice was more gentle now. And when I sighed, it wasn't as heavy.

"Yeah, I kinda got that feeling too," I confessed. "I didn't want to think it was true."

"Go on, then," Saki said, pushing at me. "If you can realize that, then you can be out there talking to her. Not talking to me *about* her."

"This whole conversation was your idea," I grumped. But I let her push me up and toward the door.

"And did it work?" Sakura paused before we went out. "Did you say everything you needed to? I mostly just wanted you to know how worried I was. Also, to lodge an official complaint. You know how much I hate being on boats, what with my legs."

*Shoot.* I did know that. Though her balance was perfectly fine on land, being on the water made Saki especially nervous. But she grinned at me, and I could tell she was mostly teasing. So I nodded. "Yeah, I think I said everything. I'm not mad at you any more, anyway. Just a little peeved."

"The status quo is restored, then," Saki said with a grin. She stepped in and gave me a brief hug before turning back toward the door. "Let's go see how Mel is doing."

## Seventeen

## New Ground

Mel

"I have no idea what I'm doing," I said to Glacial.

The baker twisted her disheveled purple head one way, then another. "Looks fine to me, I guess."

"You guess?" I stepped back and looked at the hearts myself, exasperated. "After the kind of press coverage we've been getting, this event has to be perfect! No guesses!"

When I turned to Glacial again, she just shrugged. The gesture let loose a cloud of cocoa powder from her apron. Another thing I'd need to clean up. "This isn't really my thing. It's more Saki's thing. She'd know."

"*What* isn't your thing?" I asked, exasperated. "Running a café? Hosting an event?"

"Well, that, and . . . hearts," Glacial said, the way a small child might say, *baths.* "Oh, good, I think I hear her coming."

I followed her gaze to the kitchen door, and relief washed over me when I recognized the shadow witch coming in. Seeing her brother behind her was a little more complicated.

It wasn't that I wasn't happy to see him—quite the opposite, actually. And he looked very healthy, aside from scowling a bit, so that was good. In fact seeing him was also kind of a relief, because it gave me something else to fixate on. Instead of a pit of anxiety in my stomach, now there was a cloud of butterflies.

*Does he know what I was going to say last night? What does he think of it? He must think I'm so silly, actually falling in love with him when this all should have been a game.*

*Wait—did I just say love?*

Needless to say, my cheeks were beet red by the time the siblings joined us in the dining area. I just couldn't bring myself to meet Ryuko's gaze. Sakura must have noticed something was up, because after briefly touching base and planning our next steps to prepare, she pulled me over to the couch nook with her.

"Let's go over the tea selection," she said, as an excuse. But then as we took our seats, she added, "And let's talk about everything *aside* from the event tomorrow, Mel. How are you doing?"

"Me?" I hesitated as I finally looked up and met her big blue eyes. Her gaze was extremely steady, and I willed myself to feel some of that confidence too. *After all, Mel, you wanted to throw yourself into life,* I reminded myself. *Don't get scared now.*

Half surprised at myself for coming up with such helpful advice—and with nary a fairy godmother in sight!—I cleared my throat and said, "Well, if you're asking if I'm sick, I think

I'm actually fine. Trent really went above and beyond with the healing. He even gave me something for my hip when it gets sore. Aside from that . . . I guess I feel worried I'm making a fool of myself, mostly."

"With the event?" Sakura asked daintily, pouring me a cup of tea.

"Yes, that. And other things too. Like—like yesterday, getting myself dumped in the lake like that. I mean, all the boaters in the club say it has to happen some time, and you just climb back in your boat and keep going, but . . ." I realized I was rambling and let my voice trail off.

When Saki handed me the cup, she had a knowing smile. "I think that's good advice for things that aren't boating, too." After taking a moment to savor her own cup of tea, she went on, "I don't think you're making a fool of yourself at all, Mel. This is the first time any of us have done anything like this. I'll bet you it's the first time anyone in Belville's even seen something like what we're trying to do. Even in a city, this would be a unique event," she added, with a pointed look at me.

I understood: she thought I was being too hard on myself, no matter where I lived. "You're probably right about that," I admitted with a small laugh. "It just feels like I should know more."

"I don't believe in 'should's," Sakura said lightly. "Unless they're about tea. I think this tea should be steeped just a tiny bit more, don't you? Anyway," she continued, which was good because I really don't know the first thing about tea, "We all, all four of us, are doing the best we can. And sometimes that doesn't look like what we expected. Take me, with that article." Her voice dropped, and she set her hand on mine earnestly. "I apologize to you, sincerely, for overstepping my bounds—and for letting that article take you by surprise. The truth is, I had Leo over a few days ago to do an interview about the event, and I was the one to help her draw up some pictures. I didn't intend to keep you out of it—it just ended up that way, since you were at work. I also didn't intend to make you and your relationship the focus of the article, either."

"I've been around enough to get it," I reassured her, but my voice was a little mumbly. "I know how the news can be sometimes. It *does* make for a very good story."

"You are more than a story. And so is Ryu, and so is whatever relationship you have—whatever it looks like," Saki said firmly. "I'll admit I've gotten excited and carried away by it all, by how well you two were getting along. I've got a sisterly vested interest, you could say. But as Ryu just reminded me, me being interested doesn't give me—or Leo—any right to put any pressure on either of you."

"I thought . . . wasn't that the whole point?" I asked hesitantly. "I mean, the article could actually be really good, as far as the original plan goes. With Ryuko getting out of participating in the auction by saying he's with me now, and all. People will definitely believe that now."

"Plans can change," Saki said, looking at me solemnly. "Do you want to change the plan, Mel?"

*Yes,* I thought. *I want to go back and never have lost the tea in the first place. I want to be safe, and good at my job, and going to my club meetings each night uninterrupted by all this crafting and arguing and worry.*

But that wasn't exactly what Sakura was asking. And—didn't it sound a little dull?

"I—I'm not sure," I said cautiously. "I think it's really Ryuko who's at stake. He could make the call."

Saki tilted her head. "Maybe that was true in the beginning, but I don't think that's what had you out there rowing on the lake in winter winds."

"Paddling, really. It wasn't that bad," I said automatically. Then, biting my lip, I explained, "My family still keeps an eye on Belville news, since they feel attached to it, having lived here. And I haven't—told them anything about this. I suppose if I'd wanted to really go incognito or something, I should have just moved somewhere different, but it was so convenient to come to Belville, with the cottage and the job post, it felt like it was meant to be somehow. And it's not that I don't talk to my family any more, I do, it's just that ever since—ever since—well, I know I should probably tell them everything, just as a matter of course, but I *don't*, because life is so complicated, and that article—"

"It doesn't fit the narrative they know?" Sakura's mouth turned up at the corners as she poured a new tea. "Here, try this one instead. And don't feel bad, Mel. We all create stories of our lives for others. Especially when we're in the middle of a big change, and we can't see the end yet."

"Thank you," I sighed as I accepted another cup. "Seriously, Saki—thank you."

"You can thank me by dropping 'should' out of your vocabulary," she said. "And also by giving me your honest opinion of this tea. Do you like it?"

"I do, actually," I said, inhaling rose and tasting cinnamon as I took comfort from my tea cup.

"Oh, good. It's one of Red's new blends, and I wasn't sure how well it'd go over. Sometimes she can get awfully experimental," Sakura said fondly. "So, then. What are we going to do?"

"About my family?" I kept my tea up by my face, hiding

behind its warm scent. "I don't know. They haven't gotten in touch with me. I guess there's a chance they didn't notice."

"But you don't actually believe that," Saki surmised, and the twisting in my stomach agreed with her. "Is this maybe why you're making Glacial, of all people, try to make the decorations perfect?"

I giggled in spite of myself. "I *am* getting a little over my head about it all. It's just all a . . . lot."

"True. And I certainly sympathize with wanting the event to be perfect. Just tell me what you need, Mel, and I'll see if I can get it done."

It struck me that this was a pretty big offer, from a shadow witch who was powerful enough to levitate two full-grown, sopping-wet people in the air for an indefinite amount of time while also magically steadying and propelling a boat. Definitely the kind of power you think about before calling on. I took a deep breath and thought. What did I want? Well, what I really wanted was to fix things with Ryuko. Or start things with Ryuko? Or finish them? Maybe what I wanted most was clarity about him and where we stood . . .

. . . and yet her brother was the one thing Sakura hadn't really asked me about. I suddenly got the feeling that that wasn't by accident. As I met her gaze and she smiled back casually, I had the sense that she knew exactly what she was doing. She was trying to clear everything else out of the way so that we could fix things on our own.

Or my feelings for him were so obvious they didn't bear discussing.

Unable to help blushing, I tried to refocus. And to my surprise, I found myself confessing.

"I don't know if Ryuko told you," I began, "but last year, I developed this serious allergy and had a bit of an accident, and I spent two seasons in a clinic, recovering. I'm very lucky. I could have died, or not have turned out as able as I am now, but—the treatment worked, and of course I know now to be careful. I guess what I'm saying is last year was a lot, and a lot of things changed. *I* changed. And so did my relationship with my family. I wanted to prove to them—and to me—that I can still do this on my own. I thought that 'this' would be my new job fixing the post office here, and maybe it will be, in the long term. But since the article is out . . ."

"The event tomorrow is another opportunity?" Saki finished.

I nodded. "That's what I really want. I want it to be proof."

The shadow witch broke into a smile. "That'll be easy. Mel, have you considered that it already *is* proof?"

I didn't totally understand what she meant by that at the time, I'll admit. But I didn't really have to: just her enthusiasm was infectious. After trying one more tea blend and chatting a little more, I was starting to feel more like my old self. Like I had on that first night, excited about the possibility of the event—not crushed with concern about everyone involved or meeting fictitious expectations. I'm not totally sure how Saki did that. But I think just talking to her helped remind me that this event *was* an opportunity. And it could be a really neat one.

Aside from the part about auctioning off her brother's time, of course.

But I managed to set aside my feelings about that and truly focus. The rest of the evening was a complete blur. By the end of the night, all the centerpieces were up, the tables were set, the guest list checked and place cards arranged. A few gift baskets and other items to be auctioned off had been dropped off—my friends at Belville Boaters had put one together, and Abi delivered a massive one from Lavender's Tavern. Glacial had finally decided on her menu, and had managed to buy all the ingredients she needed—including some very fancy cases of wine that made me wince when they came in. The bakery case and sales counter had been polished until they shone, and every picture frame and knickknack had been dusted and placed with care. The upstairs was still cordoned off—after the setback with the banister, we all decided not to bother opening the upstairs. Instead, we'd have a cozy setup on the first floor. We did hang the mobiles from the balcony—Sakura insisted on doing that herself. By the end of the night, the only things left to do—aside from actually cooking and serving food—were collect our order of fresh flowers and tend to the last-minute mishaps that always occur right before a new event begins.

Somewhere in all the bustle of cleaning and decorating, Glacial had made us all pizza and cookies. So when it was time to go home at last, I stood there with Sakura and Ryuko by the front door, munching a cookie, lingering in the warmth before going out into the dark night. I felt full and tired and still a tiny bit nervous, but so much more prepared.

Of course, though, the moment Sakura declared that she was going to confer with Glacial one more time and that we should go home without them, the butterflies were back in my stomach again.

Probably shouldn't have gone for that last cookie.

"I'll walk you to your place," Ryuko said gruffly, before I could come up with any words.

"Oh," was my brilliant reply. He held the door open and I slid out past him, trying not to think too hard about what it had been like to be leaning into his chest. Once we were outside

121

and the fresh wind hit my face, I managed to gather a few more wits together. "You really don't have to."

"It's what a gentleman would do, right?" Ryuko hunched his shoulders against the cold, but he also—for just a moment, just faintly—smiled at me.

"Right." I smiled, too, thinking that if that's how he wanted to be, I could play along. It *was* awfully easy to talk to him. Or tease him. Even when he was at his grumpiest. As we started off down the sidewalk, I asked, "So is this going to be a thing with you now, before every decision you make? 'What would a gentleman do'?"

He laughed, a short, surprised sound. "Probably not. Too much effort."

"Yeah, but don't you say that about everything?"

"Maybe. But this time I mean it."

"I guess that's fair, seeing as thinking like a gentleman got you dunked in the lake."

"*That* time was worth it," Ryuko said, glancing sideways at me.

I snorted. "Are you sure? I didn't get the impression that sleepovers with your sister at Trent's Hut were your favorite thing in the world."

"Definitely not," he growled.

"So, not worth it, then."

"Worth it," he insisted, turning more fully to face me this time, "because if you had drowned, I wouldn't have been able to live with myself."

"Oh." Warmth bloomed inside my chest, despite the night. "Well, I—I guess it *would* have been your fault, if anything bad had happened. Seeing as you were the one who rammed me, and all."

"What?" He missed a step, and then he laughed again. "I thought you were supposed to be some ace rower. Why couldn't you have maneuvered out of the way?"

"I like *paddling*. There's a difference. And you were distracting me!"

"No more than *you* were distracting me. I wouldn't have even been out there if it wasn't for you."

"Well, I probably wouldn't have been out there alone if it wasn't for *you*," I shot back. I had meant it to be playful, but it came out a little too close to the mark. I gulped, embarrassed. Fortunately, we were already pretty close to my house.

But *un*fortunately, Ryuko wasn't letting it go. He paused at my little front gate. "What does that mean, Mel?"

"I—just that—oh, I don't know," I babbled, eyeing my front door. Seriously, how many times was I going to *almost* confess to this guy how I really felt? All the butterflies in my stomach were about to revolt, and my heart just couldn't take it any more. "Just, you know, this whole thing with the café and Saki. And you. Not that I'm mad about it at all," I added. "And I'm not upset I'm involved, really. I've actually had a great time. But now I'm super tired, and there's a lot to do tomorrow, so I think I better just head to bed."

Ryuko was silent for what felt like a really long time. His voice sounded a little more strained than usual when he finally did speak—but maybe that was just my own nerves talking. "Are you going in to the post office tomorrow?" he asked.

"No, it's my day off," I answered. "Lucky, right? I mean, I would have taken it off anyway. Just to be there, just in case. Are you? Going into your work, I mean?"

He shook his head.

"Oh, okay. So, then—I'll see you tomorrow, at the café?

Bright and early, probably."

"Yeah," he said. "I'll probably be there when you get there."

"Or I'll get there even earlier," I said quickly. I could not, for the life of me, have told you where that sudden competitive streak came from. "Since, you know, I always get up so early. For work. And lately you've been used to sleeping in."

"Is that how it is?" He grinned at me, a crooked grin I could just barely see by the streetlight. "Alright, fine. We'll see who gets there first."

# Eighteen

# What I Like About You

Ryuko

On the big day, I was in the café first. Aside from Sakura and Glacial, obviously. But they didn't count. And while they huddled in the kitchen dithering about what decoration to put on the cupcakes, I waited at the counter for Mel.

She came in through the front doors, bundled up in a long coat. It was after sunrise, but only just. It was clear why she was a little late. Her hair was carefully brushed, down, with a headband that sparkled with red gems. When she bent to take off galoshes, she put on fancy little shoes with a low heel. And when she took off her coat, she was wearing a knitted crimson dress that hugged her long, curvy figure.

125

"You're late," I told her, because I couldn't tell her the truth, which was *you're beautiful.*

She turned to face me slowly. She wasn't surprised; she'd known I was there. The café lights were low, but I knew elves have good vision in the dark. I wasn't trying to scare her, anyway. Just maybe disarm her a little, the way she had me.

But as she walked over to the counter, she was picture perfect. Of course. "I'm fashionable," she informed me. "And you, I bet, were dragged here. Saki was probably scared you'd run."

I recognized the running joke, but was too off-guard to do anything with it. Instead I slid her a cup of coffee. "Don't worry, I didn't make it. Saki did. She's in the back. It makes sense you'd be late," I couldn't help but add. "Ladies have a lot of prep work to do."

One eyebrow arched, and then she was grinning too. "Ladies like to call it 'dressing up.' Or 'pampering,' if they're really insufferable."

"Two guesses as to which one you are," I said, watching her steadily.

Her gaze flicked my way as she sipped her coffee. "You know, gentlemen usually dress up too. You could try it some time."

I chuckled. It was a casual shot that hit home. I *was* dressed up, for *me*, anyway. Clean shirt, knit sweater, dark pants. It had taken some time to rustle up a sweater that didn't have any holes from the laundry bins that served as my closet these days, since I'd given up my room for Saki and Glacial to share. From the small, sweet smile Mel gave me as she set down her cup, I could tell she knew that.

"Well, isn't this pleasant," Sakura declared as she emerged from the kitchen. "You two don't know how lucky you are. You don't have to worry about the menu. Ryu, is there any of that coffee left? Please don't tell me you gave it all to Mel."

"We're in a café," I informed her. "If you want coffee, make more."

Across the counter, Mel laughed. "Saki, I didn't mean to take your drink. If you like, I—"

"Oh, don't pay any attention to me," said Sakura, waving a hand above her head. She was so short she could disappear behind the big coffee machines otherwise. "Mornings aren't my strong suit. Once things are running smoothly in the café, I plan on making Glacial do the early business. She's always up to bake, anyway. You could join her, Ryu!"

"Pass," I said, still watching Mel. "I told you. I'll do the carpentry. I won't talk to customers."

"Are you going to make that a full-time thing, then?" Mel asked me, refocusing on my face. "I think you could do really well, actually. I don't think I got a chance to say it last night, but the centerpieces are gorgeous. And I don't care what Dusty says—all the shelves seem perfectly level to me."

Her smile had me ready to say I was planning on taming lions full-time. Her joke about Dusty made me roll my eyes.

Saki, armed with coffee, took her chance to leap back into the conversation. "For the record, I agree. And Mel, you probably didn't get a chance to say it because you two are always too busy fighting. Or flirting," she said, with a totally unnecessary wink. "So, before you start doing that all over again, let's make a plan. I have to run out and get the flowers myself—I made all the arrangements already. Trent will be here later. He *really* doesn't do mornings. He—"

"Why's Trent coming?" I interrupted. I half suspected Saki of arranging medical checks or something.

"If you'd waited, you'd know," my sister retorted. "As I was going to say, Trent's coming to try out the acoustics. I was thinking," she continued, turning to Mel with a much brighter tone, "that since the entertainment—the auction—is going to be interrupted, according to our plan, we ought to have something planned as back up. Just so there's not an awkward silence, you know?"

Mel grinned at my grimace. "So Trent is your back-up entertainer?" she asked.

Saki nodded. "He plays mandola. It's a stringed instrument, kind of like a cross between a fiddle and one of those guitars so popular in Brass. He's actually quite good, I think."

"You might be biased," I muttered.

But of course, Saki ignored me. "Anyway, he'll have to be good, because he's the only musician I could get on such short notice. I was thinking, since the upstairs is still empty, I'll make a big show of lifting some of the furniture up there. Then people will have space to dance!"

I saw immediately where this was headed. "I'm not dancing."

"Let's not get distracted from our plan," Saki said, in her totally un-reassuring I'm-ignoring-you voice. "Ryu, I need you to help Glacial with some moving stuff around in the kitchen."

I wanted to protest. Wasn't Glacial strong enough already? Particularly given her supposed past as a mercenary?

But Mel cleared her throat and spoke up. "Saki, I had a thought. The one thing we might have forgotten is candles. Do you have any? Because if you don't, I was going to offer to run to the candle store for some."

"Oh, perfect!" Saki was already all over it, her hands clasped. "Just tell Lumi I'll pay for anything you get. I can't believe I forgot that—I can't wait until next year when we just have these things on hand and the whole thing has become second nature.

Can you focus on floral or fruity scents? And red, white, or dark colors?"

"That was my plan," Mel said, smiling shyly.

She wasn't looking at me, but I smiled anyway. She really was good at decorating and helping with events. It was clear she didn't want to leave her job at the post office any time soon, but at least she'd be able to throw perfect parties for all those clubs she insisted on joining.

Saki elbowed me. From her look, I could have sworn she'd caught me thinking about Mel's future—like I had any right to it. Mel herself had already gone over to put on her coat and head out the door. I glared at my sister and trudged back to the kitchen.

Rumors aside, Glacial's really good at whatever she focuses on doing. She was hyper-focused on cooking, so most of my work was just to stay out of her way while shifting boxes of ingredients. It wasn't bad, and it passed the time, at least. By the time I was done, Mel had come back with a huge basket from Lumi, the candlemaker. She was busy putting candles on each table.

It wasn't until that exact moment, watching Mel move around the decorated tables in her red dress, that I really realized that the auction was that *night*. And I'd have to be on *stage*.

Well, sort of. I'd convinced Saki there was no way we could build a stage in the café, thankfully. Instead, she was planning to use the counter as a focal point. We'd stand behind it during the main event.

Suddenly, I felt like a loaf of bread waiting to be sold. My throat was dry as old crumbs.

"Hey." Saki came up behind me, still in her puffy coat. She'd only just returned with the flowers. "You look like you're getting nervous."

"Something like that," I admitted, my eyes glued to Mel.

"Me-el," Saki called, and I nearly elbowed her back just for that. I didn't want to be caught staring. Or nervous. "When you're done with the candles, can you help Ryu with his speech? Trent just got here, and he's going to help me put out the flowers. Oh, and don't forget to have a little lunch, you two!"

She sailed away, and Mel set down her last candle carefully before coming over to me. "Speech, huh?"

"Don't tell me." My voice came out rougher than I meant it to. "A gentleman would have already written something."

Mel just laughed. "Actually, I totally forgot that Saki wanted you to make one. I guess it makes sense, right? I mean, we do have to give people *some* kind of explanation. Come on." She waved me over to sit at a nearby table.

On impulse, I pulled out my carpenter's pencil and notebook. And then sat frozen.

"You know," Mel said, with a glance around the café like we were kids sharing a secret, "you don't really have to make a speech if you don't want to."

I don't know what it was, but those words turned my whole attitude around. If she was going to admit defeat, I was going to say something even if it killed me.

"I said I would, so I will," I decided, tightening my grip on my pencil.

"Did you ever technically say you would, or did Saki just decide that?" Mel asked, amused.

"Doesn't matter." I glanced at her. "It's the gentlemanly thing to do."

"Don't forget to list off the reasons you love Mel," Saki called, as she floated by with a few flowers. Trent followed behind her with an entire barrel. "People love that kind of thing!"

I turned to Mel, who was already blushing. "You *really* don't have to do that."

"I do," I insisted. "You deserve it, Mel."

She pursed her lips. "Well, I don't know about that. Who are you to say what I deserve?"

"I *will* say I don't love that self-deprecating attitude," I told her, chastising. But at the same time, I began to make my list. As I wrote, I said more quietly, "But I *do* like your wit."

"Wit?" Mel's eyes were as big as the tea cups.

"And the way you told Saki you didn't think you were the right choice to help with the auction, but then most of the best ideas were yours," I added, making a point of not looking at her.

"Best?"

"Also the fact that you've been working as hard as anyone on this event, even though you have a real job on top of all this."

"Are—are you sure?"

"And who goes out rowing to clear their head at this time of year? It's honestly cute."

"*Cute?*" she squeaked.

"Plus," I said, finally looking up, "you can't draw hearts."

This broke the spell. She lunged forward. "You never gave me a chance!"

"I could tell," I said, doing my best to keep my cool. It felt like there was a timer going off in my head. If she kept looking at me like that, after all of this, I was going to *have* to kiss her in *five* . . .

"You could not," she retorted, adorably obtuse.

"I absolutely could." *Four* . . .

"You're not really going to say any of these things, are you?"

"Oh, I am." *Three . . . One.* I reached out, taking hold of the back of her chair, and leaned in.

A cold burst of air interrupted me. I turned just enough to see that the front door of the café had opened, and two tall figures were standing there, staring right at us.

Mel stood so fast the table rattled. "Mom? Dad?"

# Nineteen

# Big City, Small Town

Mel

Seeing my parents show up unexpectedly at the Pomegranate was like a nightmare. The kind of nightmare teenage me would have thought up, where I was about to kiss the guy I'd had a crush on forever, and then suddenly my parents were there to ask why I wasn't prepared for the test and why I'd forgotten to put on pants.

*Guy I've had a crush on?*

"Mom, Dad," I said, trying so hard to make my voice sound normal and happy that I'm sure I sounded anything but. "What are you doing here?"

"We came to see the auction, of course," my mother said. She stepped forward to hug me—something I was too in shock to really reciprocate—and then she glanced over at Ryuko. "Is this the young man you're supposedly in love with?"

"This is Ryuko," I gurgled. "He's Saki's sister—um—this is Sakura's café—she's around here somewhere—"

*Seriously, how did that shadow witch always know when to disappear?*

"Ryuko," my father echoed, as he stepped forward too. His voice had an ominous tone. I opened my mouth to head off whatever he was about to say, but he beat me to it. "I remember you now. Didn't you serve out your mandatory service with one of our media outlets a few years back?"

If before I'd been gurgling, now I was a drowned fish. My mouth snapped shut. I stared at Ryuko.

He stared back at me, nodded, and then disappeared.

Just like everyone else in the café.

I dropped back into my chair and honestly, the world went black and watery for a minute. I'm not at all sure what we said. My mother began walking around the dining area, surveying the decorations, fixing the flowers and exchanging candles, but I wasn't actually paying attention to anything she said. My father sat at the table with me. I did my best not to look at him. After all, I was upset with him. Who just comes out and says something like that to someone you're just meeting?

*Ryuko was sentenced to mandatory service?* It wasn't at all un-heard of—courts all across Belville usually gave out magically-enforced work sentences rather than jail time. Sometimes it was a few months, sometimes years, depending on the crime, but the intent was to create something positive out of a bad situation. In fact, for a lot of people, they managed to earn money and learn skills that they'd needed in the first place—or sometimes get a firsthand look at a community they'd harmed. Working for a reputable newspaper was a pretty common sentence for charges where someone had conned others, or maybe written something false on purpose. My father's companies had employed dozens of people like that over the years. There wasn't anything bad about the service itself, though it did beg the question what had happened *before* the sentence. And it also made Ryuko's suspicion of anything 'gentlemanly' make more sense.

I was curious about the details, but only vaguely. I was a lot *more* curious about where he'd gone, and if he was still in the café. And why he hadn't felt like he could tell me before. But still, it's not like we'd been divulging *all* our secrets and comparing pasts . . .

And if I'd learned anything over the past year, it's that it was the present—and the future—that mattered most.

But seriously, the person I needed to be having this conversation with was Ryuko, and he was gone. And I knew from experience there'd be no pinning him down until he decided he was ready to talk about it.

I just really, really hoped he'd be ready to talk about it soon.

In the meantime, what was I supposed to do with a critical party-expert like my mother and an unamused tag-along like my father, several hours before the big auction, with final details still to put together? Not to mention the headlining "entertainment" gone missing.

I needed a fairy godmother so badly in that moment, I'd have been unendingly grateful if even *Sakura* showed up.

But the shadow witch was still nowhere to be seen, and I had to pull things together myself. I took a deep breath and tried to think. Out of all the options available to me, what did *I* want to do?

135

"Mom, Dad," I said, straightening up. "Come on. We've done enough here, and Saki has things under control. Wherever she is. I'll take you over to Lavender's tavern and we can get some lunch. And have you seen the new dock? They rebuilt it since we moved away. The lake is really lovely this time of year . . ."

After being so quiet, it was like I couldn't stop myself from talking. But the good thing about that was that my parents never had time to protest. My father rose with me, and together we pulled my mother away from examining the mismatched china. The fresh spring air outside came as a huge relief.

Lunch was painful at first, but it soon settled into something almost familiar. News about my sister, questions about my health. Talking over Leo's article—that *was* what had brought them there. This was everything I'd feared would happen. And honestly, it wasn't *so* bad . . .

. . . Aside from them ambushing Ryuko. And him having been so cryptic to me in the first place.

But it wasn't until the three of us stood down on the shores of the lake that the subject of my love life came up again.

"Lovely view," my father said perfunctorily.

"Very charming," my mother agreed.

"Yes. I love it here." I took a deep breath, looking out over the calm waters, the reflection of the evergreen-covered hill across the lake. It was quiet and still, aside from a few fishing boats. Everyone in town was at work—as I'd expected to be. But I'd dropped everything when my parents showed up. Just like I'd been so sure I needed to prove something to them with a "successful" event, a busy career . . .

*Maybe,* I thought, *it isn't just Ryuko who's been feeling held back by his past.*

"So, you're serious about boats now?" my mother was asking.

But that wasn't what I wanted to talk about. "I really like my life here," I announced, turning to my parents. "I've kind of been afraid to show you how much. I know it's not what you expected. It isn't what I expected either. But I'm not upset about it. And I'm not settling," I added.

My parents exchanged a look. "Is this about that article?" my mother asked.

"The young man," my father added.

"The article was mistaken. It was an exaggeration," I said. "And Ryuko isn't just some 'young man.' I'm over thirty, for goodness' sake, and I'm pretty sure he is too. Neither of us is all that young any more."

"Honey . . ." my mother's tone was a warning.

"Let her explain," my father decided.

I glanced out at the lake again. I'd started this conversation. I was going to have to face up to everything it entailed. "I'm glad you both came down for the dinner tonight," I began. "It means a lot to me, and it means a lot to Sakura. Saki's my friend—you'll meet her later. This opening means a lot to her. She asked me to help because she knew I'd have good advice. And—she also asked me to help her brother, Ryuko, with something. It was mostly a joke, really."

*As much as owing a shadow witch a favor ever feels like a joke . . .*

"Anyway," I said, clearing my throat, "you read all about the auction. It was all Saki's idea, and Ryuko wasn't comfortable with it. So we figured I'd help him out of it. I'm kind of like his fall-back dance partner," I said, and I couldn't help smiling, because I knew he'd hate that comparison.

"I know you said you're grown up," my mother said, "but acting as someone's fall-back? You're better than that."

137

"I'm not better than anything," I retorted, frustrated. "I wish everyone would stop thinking like that. I'm not *too good* to work for the post office, or to live way out here in Belville, or to come to someone's rescue because their sister set them up on a date they didn't want. I'm just *me.* All I want, now that I have a second chance, is just to be *me.*"

My father opened his mouth, but for the first time in my life, I cut him off. "And I don't want to hear any judgments about Ryuko, either. He's here now, and he's *been* living here perfectly fine for several years, so it's obvious that his past is in the past and he must have done his work just fine for whatever company he was assigned to. There's nothing wrong with him and there's nothing wrong about us being friends. You don't know him now. *I* do."

Both my parents were silent for a moment, blinking at me. Then my father said quietly, "It doesn't appear to me that you are just friends."

"Well, we haven't decided yet if we want to try being anything more," I replied, a little uncertainly.

"But honey," my mother broke in, "your ideals are all well and good, but you have to remember, you could be a target. Your inheritance, for example, might be very tempting—"

"I can look after myself," I interrupted. "I do alright on my own, and—"

My mother was still talking. "Yes, you say that now, but—"

"But what?" I asked, daring her to finish that sentence. "Listen, *I* took care of my recovery. After my diagnosis and everything that happened with the accident, *I* made sure that I did all the therapy, and that I was okay. And I was hired for the job here because of *my* work record, and I moved here by myself just fine. I'm okay making my own decisions. No matter how they might turn out. And we don't *know* how they'll turn out yet, because we aren't at the end."

Silence met this, at first. I have to admit, deep down I was scared they'd just walk away. I hadn't ever said most of these things so explicitly before.

I hadn't even realized how much my old expectations and "better than"s and "should"s had been holding me back.

"Do you . . . want to stay for the auction, at least?" I asked, eventually, in a much smaller voice. "We all worked really hard on it. My friends at the boat club donated this really cute date package, and Lavender's giving away a cooking lesson . . ."

"Oh, honey." My mother hugged me, and to my surprise, my father followed suit.

"No matter how it turns out," he whispered, rather stiffly, but still sincerely, "we're proud of you."

# Twenty

## A Surprise Bidder

Ryuko

I never actually read that article Saki had Leo run. I knew that Saki felt bad and that probably meant that whatever'd been written would hurt Mel. I didn't know it talked about love. Just hearing that word made everything worse.

"You have to calm down eventually," Sakura was saying. "Just let everything out, then you can pull yourself back together. Just for tonight. Just for this event!"

We were back in the old barn behind the café, because that's where Saki had found me. But this time I wasn't leaning on a set of wheels. I was actively destroying them.

"You're going to get sawdust all over your one nice top," Saki added.

"Doesn't matter. All this junk needed to be broken down eventually anyway," I muttered, snapping a wheel in half.

"Ryu, you have every right to be upset, but—"

"How do you know?" I began making a new pile of junk to burn later. "Did you see what happened?"

"Well, no, but I can guess."

The way she said it gave me pause. I straightened up. "Saki. You knew? About Mel's . . . about Mr. de Foret?"

"Of course I did," she said, perching on an old dresser. Probably so that I wouldn't smash it. "I researched who owned the newspaper when you were sent to work there."

"You did?"

"Didn't you?"

"I had other things on my mind," I growled. I hadn't realized Saki had been so involved, even then. She'd been away, on her own journey of learning magic at the time. The thought that she'd kept tabs on me, on top of everything else, made my throat hurt. I looked up, willing myself not to react.

"You can if you want to, you know," Sakura said, very quietly. "Cry, I mean."

"It's—it's just—" I gave up. Wiping at my eyes with my arm, I went and took a seat beside my sister. "It's all such a mess."

"Of course it is. Because you didn't tell her everything from the beginning," Saki said, putting her arm around my shoulders affectionately.

I snorted, and had to wipe my face again. "What am I supposed to do? Go around telling everyone? Should I make up business cards or something?"

"Ryuko, ex-con, carpenter's apprentice," Saki giggled. "No, you don't have to do that. But some people are worth telling."

I shook my head, not wanting to think about what she was

getting at.

But she wouldn't let it go. "Think about it," she insisted. "You know that if you had told her and she was prepared, Mel would have deflected anything they had to say. You know she's like that. She *always* has something to say back to you, when you get sassy. And you know she doesn't care," Saki added softly. "Ryu, you know this isn't a big deal to her, right? If it was, she would have reacted differently."

"We don't know anything," I said, pushing her away. "Like you said. I didn't tell her. So it doesn't matter what I think any more."

"*Please,*" Saki returned derisively. "I'm sure nothing is ruined because of that one quick moment."

"There shouldn't have been anything to ruin in the first place," I argued. "Not with her. Not with *me*."

Saki threw up her hands. "Fine. If you want to be pouty, be that way. Just make sure you're in the café—and *clean*—in time for the auction later. I have to go finish setting up."

I didn't say anything. She hopped down and ran off.

And, in the silence of the empty, ruined barn, I could hear that little voice in the back of my mind that said she might be right. But I ignored it. Because Mel's father hadn't said anything that wasn't true.

The sun set and I didn't feel any better. When it really came down to the wire, though, I wasn't going to let Saki down. (After all, wasn't that what got me into this mess in the first place?)

By the time I trudged into the café, it was crowded. Seeing as Glacial had literally growled at me when I opened the kitchen door, I'd had to walk around to the front. As the door shut behind me, everyone stared.

"There he is!" Sakura sang, as though we'd planned it all along. "Right on time!"

I made my way through the tables. Every one of them was full. Of course, I noticed Mel at a table in the back corner immediately. Her parents were there too. I made sure never to look their way.

As I joined Sakura behind the main counter, I saw from the empty space that she'd already auctioned off most of the items. The place smelled like chocolate and wine, which meant that I'd missed dinner. That part didn't bother me—I hadn't planned to eat, anyway. I *was* a little frustrated with myself for cutting the timing so close, though.

But of course, Saki wasn't. She beamed up at me. "Ready?"

"As I'll ever be," I muttered.

"Stop me at any time," she said. And then she turned to the crowd and launched back into her auctioneer voice. "Alright, everyone! Thank you for making this such a fun night. And now, in the spirit of the season, here's one last game to round things out! We all know Ryuko, right? He's grouchy and quiet, but he has a heart of gold. When he heard about his little sister having this auction, he offered up his time to the biggest new donor to the café! The winner is entitled to a free meal here at the Pomegranate or any restaurant of your choice—the only catch is, you'll have to take Ryu here with you."

She turned to me with a laugh. I was a little surprised when everyone else laughed with her, like they were in on the joke. That implied they *didn't* think I was the worst part of the deal . . .

. . . But I didn't have to look at Mel and her family to know how they felt.

Saki took that moment to give me a look, and I knew she was

giving me a chance. A moment to speak up.

She hadn't yet realized that I wasn't going to.

I saw the idea settle in her eyes, and she seemed to hesitate for a moment. But then she went on. What other choice did she have?

"So," she said brightly, turning around again. "Who would like to start us off?"

I thought *no* one would, and the whole thing would end there. But then two people piped up—Red and Luca. (How weird would that have been?) Then more people shouted out bids. A few more than I'd expected, honestly. Soon there were a lot of people shouting. They all had been drinking and sounded like they were having a good time. I didn't pay any attention to who the voices came from. Until I heard one.

"I'll bid everything. Enough to cover the expansion on the second floor!"

It sounded like Mel.

Everyone stopped and turned. Probably because of her ridiculous offer. I turned because I hadn't expected to hear her speak.

"I—I'm closing it out," she said, rising slowly, almost shy. She smiled apologetically at the crowd. "Sorry to cut off the fun of bidding, everyone. But I—I just couldn't sit quietly any more."

"Are you sure?" I didn't even realize at first that the one who asked the question was me.

Mel looked right at me, and she smiled. Something lit her from above, a soft light—probably Sakura's doing, in retrospect. She looked ethereal, surrounded by hearts and flowers and all of Saki's silly teapots on the wall.

"I guess you all read Leo's article," she said, for the benefit of the room. "The truth is, it was a bit of a joke at the time. But

144

now, things are different. Before, I thought I was just doing a favor for my friend and her insufferable brother. That was until I realized, in the past few days, how smart, creative, loyal, and foolhardy that brother could be. He even jumped into the lake after me! So, yes, Ryuko. I'm sure. I'm certain, in fact. Actually, I'm one hundred percent positive that you will *not* be going on any dates with anyone else in the foreseeable future." She beamed, and everyone cheered, and then shyly she added, "Unless you want to?"

"I don't want to," I said, clearing my throat. "Go on a date with anyone else, I mean."

"Well, then, that's that, folks!" Sakura cried. "And good thing too. Here's to Pomegranate Café's newest donor!"

Another cheer went up. I could tell Saki was winding up to do her whole "lift the tables and dance" bit. Before she could give the crowd the idea to make us kiss or something, I decided to get out of there. I needed to talk to Mel. Saki had been right all along, it turned out. Talking to Mel was absolutely the answer to my problems.

I vaulted over the sales counter, ignoring the nearest tableful of diners, who honestly seemed delighted. I made my way to Mel—just Mel. I still couldn't bring myself to look at anyone else.

It was probably a good thing, then, that she was coming toward me, too. Before I could trip or run right through someone, she met me in the middle of the café.

"Come on," she said, her hands immediately on mine. "Let's go outside for a moment, shall we?"

I don't think I'd ever heard such a good idea in all my life.

145

## Twenty-One

# Won at Auction

Mel

I tugged Ryuko through the kitchen doors, past Glacial and her mountain of cupcakes, and out onto the café's cluttered back porch before I let myself think any more thoughts. When I turned to him, I could see he was as breathless as I was, and then my thoughts restarted all at once, going something like this:

*I really just did that. I'm investing with Saki, and I told the whole town I won't let Ryuko date anyone else!*

*Well, now my parents definitely can't say they're out of the loop.*

*Ryuko is so, so hot, even with that shocked look on his face . . .*

But I guess the look on my face must have been just as shocked. Because Ryuko reached out and brushed his hand against my chin, and I realized my mouth was still hanging open. This made me laugh, which made him laugh, which exhilarated me to the point where I laughed even harder.

When we finally caught our breath, he said, "That was some list, Mel. But I would've thought a lady'd be more specific."

I kissed him.

More specifically, I wrapped my arms around his neck and pulled him in before he had any chance to protest, and I met his lips with mine, hard and fast. Before that moment, I'm sure I wouldn't have ever thought I could kiss that way. But something about Ryuko just pulled it out of me. With his hands pressing at my back and his warmth beating away the nighttime chill, I could have done anything.

"Wait," he murmured, pulling back just far enough to speak. "Wait, Mel. I wanted to talk to you."

This made me chuckle. "Well, go on then," I said, nestling against his shoulder. I had a few things I needed to say, too, but they could wait just a moment.

It took a moment and more, though, for him to say something next. As my breath slowed, I listened to my heartbeat—and his. His voice rumbled up from his chest when he finally said, "I was a fool when I was a kid. All I ever thought about was being the best. By the time I was twenty, it was just me and Saki, but I still never listened to her. I got myself mixed up with a gang in Brass and I made all the money and documents they wanted. Until I finally lost the stomach for it. Didn't take too long after that to get caught, and I spent a year at the paper. Worked off the debt and scraped together enough to come here, to do basically nothing . . . Until everyone started pointing out that I'd earned a new start but hadn't actually *lived* it yet."

Ryuko paused, and I let his story settle into my brain, thinking it over. *It tracks with everything I know about him,* I thought, and somehow that was oddly comforting. I also saw immediately why he'd given me such a pained look a few nights ago when I'd talked about my stress. All that stress, exactly the same thing he was talking about now, the belief that I had to be the *best* in order to be worthy or safe . . .

And for just a moment, standing there in the cold with my arms wrapped around Ryuko, I knew exactly what a fairy godmother would have said: *darling, you're already perfectly worthy, just as you are.*

The feeling of it took my breath away, and in the silence, Ryuko spoke again. "Did you really mean it? Everything you said? Even after everything that's happened?"

This shook me from my reverie. "Of course I did. And I still do," I said, half indignant, half amused, and totally feeling sympathy for his bewilderment. "You know I wouldn't lie about something like that."

Maybe it was the word *lie* that made him falter. He sucked in another breath. "I'm sorry I didn't tell you sooner."

"It's okay," I said, and I absolutely meant it. "I mean, I really wish you had, of course, but we've had a *lot* going on. I'm really grateful you've told me now. And, to be honest—I get it. Ryuko, even though this whole afternoon was a big shock, it wasn't like I was ever disappointed in you or going to run away without talking to you or something. Mostly I was just wondering where *you*'d gone," I explained with a little laugh. "And it wasn't okay for my parents to just come out with it like that. I'm sorry for how that all went down."

"It's not your fault. But still. I should have mentioned it, because that would have explained why I was never good enough for—ow!"

I'd jabbed him in the ribs. "From here on out, that's what I'm doing to anyone who says the words 'good enough.' Or 'should.' I had to tell my parents the same thing this afternoon. All I want is to be myself—and to spend time getting to know you, the real you. You're the one who has made this week so much fun."

Ryuko gaped. "You really mean that?"

"Of course I do. I mean, you've also made it incredibly frustrating. But what's life without a few imperfections?" I grinned up at him.

He frowned back at me. "Gentlemen and ladies are perfect. That's the whole point."

"And that's why pretending to be proper was only ever just a game," I pointed out. "Ryuko, if I actually *liked* that kind of thing, don't you think I'd have stayed in the city?"

"Huh." He did actually sound surprised, and he even relaxed a little. "I never thought about it that way."

"I know, because you're always assuming the worst. But that's the beauty of new starts," I told him. "You don't have to make any assumptions any more. You get to find out new truths for yourself."

Ryuko's fingertips along my chin gently urged me to look up, and when I did, this time *he* kissed *me*. He moved more slowly than I had, cupping my face, savoring the moment. The realization that for him this really *was* a revelation—that it was a revelation for *both* of us, in fact—sent happy shivers racing down my spine. So did the way he moaned softly when I ran my hands down his back.

"Hey," Glacial yelled at us from the kitchen. This time when we were interrupted, I didn't jump away. We stayed entwined as she explained, "Saki wants you to come in. She says if you don't, you don't get food."

"We'll go somewhere else," Ryuko growled.

To my surprise, Glacial growled right back. "You'll go in and you'll like it, or you'll be sleeping with one eye open from here on out."

I laughed. "We'll go in and play nice. It's Pomegranate's big opening day," I reminded Ryuko, smiling. "And besides, everything worked out. What have we got to be mad about?"

As he looked at me, it was heavenly to watch his glare melt. "I haven't eaten anything yet," he admitted reluctantly.

"I bet you even skipped lunch, and then refused to come in for dinner," I observed. "And that's too bad, because Glacial's cheese fondue was amazing. Alright then, that's settled. In we go. How bad can it be?"

## Twenty-Two

# *Valentine's Magic*

~∽∾∿~

Ryuko

To be honest, from the moment Mel stood up and stopped the auction to say she actually wanted me, it was like I was in a haze. (I might still be in that haze.) It was hard to believe. But the way she leaned into me made it hard to doubt.

When we walked back into the café together, it was like I was seeing everything clearly for the first time. Saki and Trent playing music, Glacial in her kitchen, the townsfolk already dancing. None of it was scary. And—it *had* been frightening before, in a way I never wanted to admit. But with Mel holding my arm in hers, I could have faced dragons.

Nobody made a big deal. Trent, sitting up on the counter

151

I'd spent an hour polishing, kept playing his goofy-looking mandolin. The dance was high-spirited and fast, and everyone was grinning as they tried the steps or just watched. No one really noticed us. Except Saki, naturally.

She was sitting up next to Trent, but she leaned back and then swiveled around to talk to us behind the counter.

"So, is it a happy Saint Valentine's Day, then?" she asked, her eyes twinkling as she looked us over.

"In the end. Very much so," Mel said, with a smile up at me. It was a little hard to hear her under all the noise, but her smile was beautiful.

"Good. Although I was thinking, Ryu," said Sakura, "maybe it wouldn't be so bad if you kept smashing things in the barn. If you get it cleared out and fixed up, then we can let Glacial live there! After all this, she definitely deserves a raise. Did you try her cupcakes?"

Cupcakes, nothing. Mel wasn't distracted. "You were smashing stuff?" she asked me.

"If I fix it up?" I asked Saki. "How skilled do you think I am?"

"Exactly as skilled as you need to be," Saki said, leveling me with a pointed look. "I think it's a great next step. Dusty can help too, of course, and we'll pay you. Right, Mel? As our not-so-secret investor, you get a say, too."

"Well, I don't know about the protocol here . . ." Mel was clearly still a little left behind, but she recovered and grinned at me anyway. "But yes, I think he'll do."

There was a break in the music and a bunch of clapping, which distracted Saki. I pulled Mel into my arms. "I just got upset with myself and needed an outlet, that's all. I *wasn't* looking for a new job."

"I get that," she said, angling her head up in a way that

made me think of kissing her again. "But would you enjoy the challenge?"

"The challenge?" I repeated. I hadn't thought of it that way at all. I'd thought of it as impossible. But she had that look in her eye, the one that made me determined to be better than I'd thought I could be.

I cleared my throat. "Fine. I'll try it. I accept," I added, grinning slyly back at her.

"What's that?" Sakura cut in. "Did I hear that Belville's newest couple has decided to dance?"

"No," I said.

"Oh, why not?" said Mel.

I looked down at her and frowned. "Whose side are you on?"

"Oh, come on," she replied, tugging me around the counter. "There are no 'sides' at the Pomegranate Café. Everyone's worthy in love."

Before I knew it, I was holding Mel's hands, dancing. And there was nothing else in the world I would've rather done.

# Epilogue

## Sakura

Well, I must say, this particular matchmaking effort on my part went *much* better than the ice cream lady affair.

But I can't take all the credit, of course. Mel and Ryu did the really hard part.

Still, I was feeling very pleased for them—especially because, within two months, they were well on their way to finishing each other's sentences, and I was well on my way to having an apartment all to myself. Ryu spent most of his nights at Mel's, where I'm pretty sure he was already helping her redecorate. And progress on the barn was going so well that soon Glacial would be able to live in the loft. Between us all, I think the stress levels in Belville must have dropped by at least twenty percent!

I think the day Ryu finished insulating the upper floor is a perfect example . . .

Mel had come over after her post office shift in order to drop off some tools of Ryu's—and also to steal some crème cacao tea and a snack from the kitchen. She and I walked over to see the barn, cupcakes in hand. Lucky for us, Ryu had just decided to take a break.

"We're coming up," I warned him from the stairs, just in case.

"Good," he called back. "Mel, did you remember the screwdriver?"

"Got it here. Plus a cupcake for you—if you're nice!"

When we made it up into the empty space, Ryu accepted both from Mel with an easy grin. "Working so hard on this project for you *is* nice."

"You may have a point," she said, leaning up to kiss his cheek.

"I think it looks lovely," I decided, looking around the room. It was only a loft, of course, but Ryu had insulated it and reinforced everything that needed some help, and it would make Glacial a perfect little studio. Glacial had insisted we leave the bottom floor of the barn empty; she hoped to use it as a gym of sorts.

"You can't see all the warped beams and cracks," Ryu told me dryly.

"You just focus on that because you're too close to the project," Mel told him, making herself comfortable on the bare floor and eating her cupcake with both hands. "A gentleman knows the value of perspective."

"A lady wouldn't sit in the dust," he retorted, dropping down next to her. The two exchanged goofy grins.

I grinned too, because it was such a marvel. My big brother, smiling like he was eight years old again!

"Glad to see the two of you getting along," I observed, sitting a little more delicately, with my prosthetics to deal with. "How's the big party for the Belville Boaters coming along? What was

155

it all about, again?"

"I'm headed there after here, actually," Mel said, beaming like she'd just won a prize. "It's an anniversary party. Did you know the club has been in Belville for fifty years? Ryu's been helping me restore the original charter and some of the other old documents," she added, with a sweet look at her beau.

"In whatever spare moments I get from this ridiculous workload," he muttered. But I could tell he loved it. And I was secretly glad, too, that he was using his old archival knowledge—to see him repurposing that old passion which had once become so twisted. He didn't really know it, but that, right there, is what shadow magic's all about.

"They just had all these old documents in a closet, can you believe it?" Mel continued around another bite of cupcake. "I think nearly everyone had forgotten about them. But I've been helping them clean up a bit and redecorate for the party. It's going to be next week. Everyone in town is welcome—would you like to come? You can see what Ryu's done with the documents, and some of the really cool old canoes they've got from the old boathouse. Plus, Lavender's catering! I would have asked Glacial," she added guiltily, "but Pomegranate has been so busy . . ."

"Don't worry about it," I assured her. At least she hadn't said "should have asked." Like Ryu, it was clear our postmaster had learned to be much kinder to herself, but she still had a long way to go. Don't we all? "It's the best problem to have. Besides, since you're an official investor and all, technically *I* ought to be apologizing to *you* that we've been too busy to pay attention to what you're up to!"

"I don't know how anyone could hope to keep track," Ryuko said affectionately, looking at Mel.

Mel blushed. "You know I'm not really all that serious about that. Really, giving that money to the café was just the best thing to do with it, all 'round."

"You say that," I said, because she *had* said it before, and often. "But you know that you're involved in Pomegranate now no matter what, right? Through thick and thin. You'll always be our events coordinator."

"Events coordinator!" Mel chuckled. "I do like that title."

"Like you need another one," Ryuko murmured. She nudged him, and he pretended to be fascinated by the remains of his cupcake.

"And we'll be having tons of events, don't you worry," I added. "After the success of the Valentine auction, how could we not?"

Ryuko snorted. "You'll have to get Glacial some help in the kitchen, then. And convince her not to be so scary."

"Glacial isn't scary at all!" I protested. But I had to admit, I did know that my friend intimidated strangers sometimes. She had a lot of secrets—some I knew, some I didn't. And one in particular had to do with love . . .

"Don't," Ryuko said, interrupting my thoughts.

"Don't what?" Mel asked, looking interested.

"That's her matchmaking face," he explained.

"Oh dear," said Mel.

"Don't you dare," Ryu added.

"You have to admit, the last time wasn't very smooth," Mel reminded me.

I beamed. "Oh, don't be silly. You two ended up just fine, didn't you?"

They couldn't argue with that. After all, we shadow witches are very often right.

# About the Author

Elle adores happy endings, fairy tales, and above all, learning new things. As a historian and educator, she believes in the value of stories as a mirror for complicated realities. She currently lives in New Jersey with a grumpy tortoise and a three-legged cat.

Find more stories set in Belville at ellehartford.com. And while you're there, sign up for Elle's newsletter to get bonus material like a map of the Pomegranate, free short stories, and extra epilogues!

**And *stay tuned!* More stories from the Pomegranate will be on their way soon. In the meantime, if you loved this one, Elle and Sakura will be eternally grateful if you left a review!**

**You can connect with me on:**

🌐 https://ellehartford.com

**Subscribe to my newsletter:**

✉ https://beyondwriting.eo.page/newslettersignup

# Also by Elle Hartford

If you loved your time in Belville, and you like mysteries, you're in luck! The Alchemical Tales is a cozy mystery/cozy fantasy series centered around Red, the alchemist with the nosy dog. You can get a set of free prequel short stories by signing up for my newsletter, or you can check out the first novel in the series:

**Beauty and the Alchemist**
In this magical mix-up of fairy tales and murder, Little Red Riding Hood solves the mystery at the heart of Beauty and the Beast . . . *What does it take to overcome a curse?* Alchemist Red and her friends will need all the help they can get to solve a crime and uncover the truth!

https://books2read.com/beauty-and-the-alchemist